THE SET-APART PLACE

BRANDI DANIELLE

Aphratah
Publishing

Festus, Missouri

DEDICATION

to my deer let loose

CONTENTS

PROLOGUE

The Mighty Ones are One, One with many functions.

CHAPTER ONE

THE CLASH OF DISCORD

W isdom and Discipline were not satisfied with the balance between good and evil. They loved the good and hated all that was evil. After the clash between these two forces, good versus evil, the Heavenlies were created to house all that was good. The Earth was created too, but it was laid waste, for it had become home to all that was evil.

Shalom did not like that the Earth housed evil and wanted to destroy it. Beauty wanted to destroy the evil too but save the Earth. Beauty liked that the evil was sentenced to a place of separation, but its location created an eyesore within the Heavenlies.

CHAPTER TWO

THE EARLY DAYS

Day One

Purpose came forth as the Mighty Ones hovered over the Earth. They said, "Let there be light," and there was. They said the light was good and separated it from the darkness.

Day Two

Although the Heavenlies were now off-limits to evil, Shalom was still concerned that pride, jealousy, greed, and lying would try to regain a foothold there. Were this to happen, it would cause a detrimental breach. The Mighty Ones therefore established a dome that secured the line of separation. This caused all that was evil to be bound solely upon the Earth. Because light had been spoken into the Earth, evil had to share its residence with good. And evil was not happy.

Day Three

The good that resided upon the Earth desired friendship. Knowing this, the Mighty Ones began to prepare an environment where friendship could grow. They spoke and waters under the dome were gathered into their place, causing dry land and seas to appear. And just like that, beautiful-colored grasses, nutritious plants, vines, and fruit trees also began to appear and beautify the once barren landscape of Earth.

Day Four

To help these things grow and multiply, they needed an energetic force to provide them with fuel to thrive. So, the Mighty Ones appointed a Sky Clock to govern the amount of time that light would touch the Earth during its day, and the amount of time that light would touch the Earth during its night. This Sky Clock was made up of two great lights and star lights. The Greater Light ruled the day; the Lesser Light ruled the night, sharing its presence with the star lights. The Sky Clock determined signs, seasons, days, and years.

Day Five

After the seas, grasses, plants, vines, and fruit trees were created, and after the Sky Clock was appointed as an energy source, the Earth was now ready for more good to be introduced into it. Taking into consideration that good would eventually be all that was housed upon the Earth, the Mighty Ones decided that the next good created would be brought forth on day five, and it would be called *the living*.

From the smallest to the largest, and everything in between, from the colorful to the not so colorful, uniquely designed fish were brought to life and were instructed to be fruitful and multiply between the boundaries of the shorelines, under the waters, which were called seas.

Beautiful birds were given life too – birds with wings to fly high into the sky and birds with wings that stayed close to the Earth's ground; birds that sang harmonious melodies and birds that were quiet. The Mighty Ones saw that Their creation was good, and all were blessed and instructed to be fruitful and multiply.

Day Six

The Mighty Ones did not stop with the fish or the birds – beasts of the field were also created and given life. Cattle, horses, deer and elephants, gorillas, koala and grizzly bears, lions and leopards, dogs, and cats. The list went on and on. Every magnificent creature that the Mighty Ones desired upon the Earth was created and marked among *the living*. The Mighty Ones saw that this was good and blessed the beasts of the field while instructing them to be fruitful and multiply.

Chapter Three

THE DOMINION OVERSEERS

The Mighty Ones also desired to create overseers that would express Their image by governing the dominion of *the living* and rightly ruling on Their behalf. Therefore, on the same day as the beasts of the field were created, living males and females were created too, and they were given the role of dominion overseers.

The Mighty Ones blessed the dominion overseers and told them to be fruitful and multiply. They were also given the Instructions for Life and were told why it was important to follow them.

Live life loving the One Who gives it to you, was the first and most important instruction. They were told that if they lived their life in this way, favor would be upon them and they would prosper, as it was meant for them.

The second instruction was to keep the *Creator's Appointments*. These were set-apart times. They included a time of communion with their Maker at the opening and closing of each day. A weekly day of rest was also appointed, as well as a monthly renewal day and a day of celebration which was to be joyfully observed at the head of each new year. The dominion overseers were told that honoring these appointments would ensure that they would keep growing in Heavenly knowledge, understanding, discernment, and – most importantly – discipline and wisdom.

The third instruction provided was to always follow *the Good Way.* This included valuing all life, treating others with dignity and care, while filling the Earth with acts of kindness and compassion. By observing this instruction they would be blessed and grow in the favor of their Maker.

The fourth instruction given was to only partake in a *diet of life,* by putting only what is good into the soil of their beings. This included consuming a plant-based diet consisting of fruits, vegetables, seeds, nuts, grasses, and grains. And just as they were to eat a plant-based diet, they were also instructed to put these same things back into the soil of the Earth, continuing the cycle of good life upon it.

The fifth and final instruction they received was to *be set-apart from evil.* And by doing this, the dominion overseers would cause the works of darkness to diminish. The works of darkness would then eventually be destroyed.

Chapter Four

DOMINION DOWNFALL

Sadly, over time, the dominion overseers began to walk in disobedience to the Instructions for Life that they had been given. No longer were they living life loving the One Who gave it to them, and neither were they showing up for their Creator's Appointments. This caused discipline and wisdom to be far from them, and while they continued to turn their backs on following the Good Way, kindness and compassion could no longer be detected amongst them.

Refusing to grow in nutritional intelligence, the dominion overseers were no longer consuming a plant-based diet. This caused their potential to grow dim.

They were multiplying, but doing so by mingling with all that was evil. And although they had been given instructions on how to till the soil and grow gardens that would sustain them with good food, the Earth's soil was now being laid to waste. It had been left barren by those who decided to neglect rather than nurture all the good that had been given them. Rebellion was flourishing.

CHAPTER FIVE

A BROKEN HEART

All the Heavenlies were watching from above as it became harder and harder to distinguish the dominion overseers from the evil that also resided upon the Earth. The Mighty Ones' heart was broken. The gift of living had been taken for granted and was being discarded for a self-centered, self-indulgent lifestyle.

The Mighty Ones decided that the evil upon the Earth had become too influential among the dominion overseers. Just because they had been made in Their image, this did not guarantee that the dominion overseers would automatically choose to rule justly. As they were created with free will, the dominion overseers had to make the choice to do good to overthrow anything that was not.

CHAPTER SIX

THE MASTER'S GARDEN

The Mighty Ones knew that choosing a set-apart lifestyle was not easy for the dominion overseers, when all they had ever known was a shared environment mixed with evil. And although evil had remained upon the Earth, this did not negate the strength and ability of the Mighty Ones to bring forth their intents and purposes to fruition upon it, which were to permanently destroy the works of darkness. Therefore, taking all things into consideration, They decided that the Earth needed a set-apart being, in a set-apart place.

The Mighty Ones could have wiped out the dominion overseers and started over. Instead, they decided to show compassion towards them. They sent the Master Gardener to Earth to create something new, and this new thing was such a sight to see! No being had ever witnessed anything like it. As it came to life, the Master Gardener placed a Fence-of-Fire around it. This fence was to keep the good in and the evil out, for this new thing was the most set-apart place in all the Earth.

CHAPTER SEVEN

FENCE-OF-FIRE

The Fence-of-Fire grew from the ground up and was no more than a few feet in height. What the fence lacked in height it made up for in heat. The Master Gardener sent out strict warnings that until further notice, all those outside the boundary of the fence were not to trespass beyond it, unless they were prepared to face strong consequences. The goal was to teach the inhabitants of the Earth how to separate the precious from the worthless. It was not that those outside the fence were worthless, or that they would never be able to enter in. On the contrary – great potential was seen in the dominion overseers, and the goal was to redeem them unto it.

Chapter Eight

THE SET-APART PLACE

The Mighty Ones' desire for a place conducive for good to grow, without the heavy influence of evil, was now coming alive! And the radiance of the most set-apart place in all the Earth was now unfolding. It was beyond compare.

The soil inside this place was different from the soil upon the rest of the Earth. It was light, airy, and workable. Its granules of dirt varied in a rainbow of colors that consisted of soft and dark earthy tones. Being rich in vitamins and minerals, and high in nutrients, every species of plant life that was growing inside this place was a viable source for food and health. And although the Set-Apart Place held an eclectic feel, it still flowed in harmonic unity. Each vine, flower, and tree had its own unique individuality and held an iridescent glow that lit up from time to time as a soft breeze would pass by. All the plant life permeated the thick oxidized air with their delightful aromas. No other place on Earth contained such an outpouring of vibrancy, vitality, and stunning beauty. The Master Gardener was very pleased.

CHAPTER NINE

THE TWO TREES

Tucked deep within, and far away from the border of the Fence-of-Fire, grew two unique trees. These two trees were distinctly different in contrast. One of the trees was by far the most grand, stately, beautifully unique, lustrous, full-of-life, and intensively vibrant tree in all the Earth.

While extending out and beyond the makeup of its physical borders, this tree exuded iridescent and translucent tones of every color known to creation, except for black. It changed from softly glowing one minute to exhibiting bold, vibrant, and loud colors the next.

Its trunk was healthy and strong, as were its sturdy and deep roots. While multiple species of trees grew and were scattered throughout the landscape of the Set-Apart Place, this tree was one of a kind. Its leaves were beautiful and varied, having twelve different shapes, and fruit hung bountifully from its branches and was produced anew every month.

Extending out for at least fifty yards, the soil surrounding the tree's base was covered in various species of worshipping wildflowers. These wildflowers danced with delight as birds and butterflies flew nearby, or up close. And they stood still and were calm as the bees buzzed by in search of nectar, which they gladly shared. The most beautiful thing of all occurred when the Master Gardener entered their proximity. They would bow and raise up, and then bow and raise up repeatedly. Then they would pop their flower heads up and stretch as far as they possibly could, reaching towards the skies. They did all this in a harmonic fashion.

Beyond the wildflowers, this majestic tree's perimeter was encircled by a beautiful, bubbling fountain of water. This fountain flowed several yards into the air, while synchronizing its motion to move in a rhythmic flow. Its sounds were soothing, full of shalom, and had the power to recharge one's vitality. Also, adding to the tree's uniqueness, the fountain flowed continually and broke out into four distinct streams. These streams diverged to water the rest of the plants, vines, flowers, grasses, and trees within the Set-Apart Place.

There were no arguments about this tree being unlike any other. It was the jeweled, crowned ornament of all that had been bordered in. It was full of life and vitality, being centered in strength and ability. It was named the Tree of Life.

The other unique tree in the Set-Apart Place was also captivating, but far from beautiful. It was completely opposite in comparison, except for its fruit, which, oddly enough, appeared very pleasing to the eye and good for food. Other than its fruit, this tree was dark. Its bark was black, brittle, and seeped a dark, sticky substance. The colors of its leaves were black with varying tones of gray, dark red, and putrid greens. This was the Tree of the Knowledge of Good and Evil.

In a place that held so much warmth, vibrancy, and life, this tree seemed so out of place. It seemed to be confused, as though it didn't know if it was supposed to be living or dying. Its fruit appeared to be full of life, but everything else appeared to be decaying; its trunk looked way too thin and weak to sustain its long, rickety, and sharp-edged branches. And, strangely enough, this tree was a bit taller than the tree that was full of life and vitality.

CHAPTER TEN

THE FIRST SET-APART BEINGS

Adam became the first male created and placed inside the Set-Apart Place. To begin with, he was only a shell, a vessel, formed out of the dust of the ground. He did not speak. He lay incomplete, until the Master Gardener stood him on his feet and spoke light into him by breathing His breath into his being. This was a momentous moment! All the Heavenlies were watching and cheering. Finally, there was a being on the Earth who not only had the Creator's breath but also carried a portion of His light.

The Master Gardener created Adam with an inner light. It was heavenly in nature, exuding outwardly from within the core of his being, causing the appearance of a glow to rest upon him wherever he went.

He was innocent, pure, stately, majestic, and dignified. He was filled with much strength and gifted with many talents. And while Adam was beautiful in appearance, the Master Gardener impressed upon his heart that he should remain humble and focus on keeping the Instructions for Life.

"For if you do these, My son, you ensure that your light will stay lit, you will stay warm, and the path in front of you will stay clear. And most importantly, you will grow in wisdom and discipline," the Master Gardener said.

Not wanting Adam to feel alone in his new world, the Master Gardener also created all kinds of animal beings that would be Adam's companion friends. And as He did with Adam, the Master Gardener spoke light into these beings, and they too were breathed upon by their Creator and given the breath of life.

"Son, I am giving you the privilege and responsibility of assigning these beings their identity names. Remember they are loved and highly favored, and I have blessed them to be fruitful and multiply. Choose wisely what you will call them."

After Adam had named all his new companion friends, he looked around to see if there would be a good match for himself. The Master Gardener knew what Adam was thinking. There was not a match for him among them. This caused Adam to be at unrest, so the Master Gardener caused him to fall into a deep sleep.

When he awoke, Adam found Eve lying by his side. He marveled and was in a state of awe. For the first time ever, Adam experienced looking outside of himself, while also having the intense feeling that his self was looking back.

The Master Gardener had uniquely designed Eve, and she was perfect for Adam in every way. In the first few moments of their time together, Adam could not stop staring at her.

"May I touch you?" he asked.

She said yes. Then Adam reached out and embraced his female, and both experienced a hug for the very first time. First to the sight and now to the touch, Adam discovered Eve's differently proportioned being, and this fascinated him.

To Adam, Eve was the most beautiful creation that the Master Gardener had created. She too exuded a glowing heavenly light. And while Adam could not stop breathing in her presence, she could not stop breathing in his.

Adam's unrest was gone. It had been replaced with great shalom and he was very grateful, for he knew that Eve was made just for him. This put his mind at ease.

The Master Gardener explained to them both that Eve had been created out of Adam's genetic code, and although they were individuals, they were also one. Their singularity was a representation of all that their oneness stood for, each having his or her own function, but together, they made up one form.

Eve was the manifestation of the abundant treasure that was too big to be limited solely to the embodiment of Adam. She *was* Adam. She was the extension of him, being the bone of his bone and the flesh of his flesh. She was the invisible of him made visible. She was everything made manifest that was found within his innermost thoughts and imaginations. She was the fountain that came forth from his well and the expression of his vessel that runneth over.

She's so beautiful! Her face, her features ... She's so perfect! I love her! I didn't know I would, but I do! I love her! Her smile – it's contagious! It makes me want to smile back. How does she do that? And her hair! Oh, I love her long and curling hair! It's beautiful, much more than mine, and so much longer than mine too. Wow, I am in love! And I am so very glad the Master Gardener made her for me!

The Master Gardener told Adam that he was to love his female but not to idolize her, because that would be putting his self above his Creator. He told Eve she was to respect her male, and if she did not, that would be her downfall, for Adam was her covering, and as she showed respect to him, she was also showing respect for herself and – most importantly – for the One Who made her.

Eve was delighted in knowing her portion. She knew the Master Gardener's plan was to fill Adam's cup of unrest with overflowing joy and shalom. And she felt complete because Adam felt complete.

My male is so handsome, so delightful and full of compassion. Together we are going to shine bright and grow in our Maker's love. I am so glad the Master Gardener made me. I am going to be the best helpmate I can be. My heart is full of joy and shalom, and I will do everything in my power to make sure my male's is too.

The Master Gardener had great love and expectation for both Adam and Eve, and He was candid with them both from the very beginning, concerning their set-apartness from the rest of the Earth.

"You are My children, My beloved, and set-apart. And when you are ready, I will teach you what you need to know about being fruitful and multiplying the seed that will come from within your union."

He also described the fall of the dominion overseers, and how He still wanted to extend compassion towards them. His desire for Adam and Eve was to raise them up in discipline and wisdom, knowing that if they adhered to His Instructions for Life, then discernment and integrity would follow.

"Keep My Instructions for Life and My favor will always be upon you, and you will prosper, as was meant for you."

The goal for Adam and Eve was to grow in the attributes and qualities that the Master Gardener held, and then, in return, they would one day teach these same things to the dominion overseers who lived on the other side of the Fence-of-Fire.

The Master Gardener wanted Adam and Eve to teach the dominion overseers discernment in knowing how wise it is to choose discipline over self-indulgence. He shared with them how He loved His creation and desired that none of it would be severed from eternal life, so He created a plan of redemption. He knew that under the right circumstances one could overcome. He knew that choosing the good over the evil only fed into more of the same. And He knew that choosing the good needed to become a habitual effort before it could ever become a habit. This is where true victory over evil would reign. This is what Adam and Eve would be taught to share with others, and this is why the Master Gardener breathed His living breath into them and gave them a portion of His light.

CHAPTER ELEVEN

WAKING UP IN THE MASTER'S GARDEN

"Eve, do you like butterflies or ladybugs better?" Adam asked from their bed.

"I like both. Go back to sleep."

While Eve's back was to him, Adam sat up in a reclining position. Having awoken a few hours ahead of her, he was now looking forward to her company.

When is she going to rise? Maybe I should just give her a little nudge, he thought.

"What about daffodils or roses? Which is your favorite?"

"I like both. Why are you waking me up with these questions? Can they not wait?"

Eve still was not moving, so Adam decided to gently pull one of her long locks of hair.

"Oh, my love, I know you like to sleep in, but I have nicknamed you my little ray of sunshine, so it would only make sense that you would live up to your name and rise with it. The Greater Light is about to greet us."

Eve rolled over to face Adam. She gave him a playful eye roll and then began to tickle him all over. Filled with delight and joy, he burst out into laughter.

Lovingly and playfully, Eve continued to tickle her male.

"Just because you nicknamed me your little ray of sunshine, doesn't mean I have to rise with it. Now, you are going to pay for waking me up."

Eve was not stronger than Adam, but for a moment he allowed himself to be held down by the weight of her being. She sat on top of him with her legs straddling his waistline, while he squirmed and laughed from the playful tickling she dished out. Allowing himself to be held down until he could no longer withstand it, Adam joyfully demanded a reprieve.

"Okay, okay, enough! Stop, I give up, I give up!"

"I love you, my male!" Eve said as she acquiesced and stopped tickling him.

"I love you too, my female!"

"My love," Eve said, with a smile on her face and much joy in her heart, "you know I prefer organic sounds of nature for my alarm clock, not twenty questions in my ear."

"The birds were chirping, my little ray of sunshine. That is our alarm clock, and they are very organic, didn't you know?"

Adam and Eve kissed on the lips and embraced in a long hug.

Waking up in the Master's garden was such a delight for them both, and even though they had nothing else to compare it to, deep down they knew it was a very special privilege to be able to wake up and experience such joy in the most beautiful place in all the Earth.

"So, my love, what are our plans going to be for the day?" Eve asked.

"Well, I am planning for us to work in the carrot and turnip patches. There are several areas that need a little attention. The soil needs to be turned over and worked to get it ready for a new crop. The rabbits keep looking at me like '*Hey, Adam, when are you going to spruce up the carrot and turnip patches? They are getting a little thin.*'"

Eve responded with much delight. "I like carrots and turnips too, my love. And yes, we do need to take care of those rabbits. It would be unkind not to."

"You are right, my love, and those patches really are getting sparse, so that will be our delightful chore for the day. We will work in the carrot and turnip patches."

"Oh, my love, wait – I did have something I wanted to do this morning. I wanted to go exploring. Would it be okay to delay work on the patches until this afternoon?" Eve asked.

"My little ray of sunshine, maybe I should change your name to the curious cat. We have plenty of time to explore after our chores are done. Let us first get our hands in the soil, and then we can venture out once that is taken care of."

"But I really had my heart set on exploring today."

Adam grabbed both of Eve's hands and proceeded to intertwine his fingers with hers. Drawing her closer he continued to speak in kindness.

"I know, my love, but I really had my heart set on working the patches today. We have time for both. Let us get this out of the way first, then we can go play," he responded.

Eve sighed then responded, "Okay, my love, you win. Have it your way."

"Aw, what's the sigh for, my love?"

"I am okay, nothing is wrong. I am just giving in," she said.

"My love, please, it's not about winning, and it's not about me having my way. This is about the Master Gardener's way. He has never led us wrong. He taught us that if we spend time taking care of His garden, it will in return take care of us. I know He is right, my love. And truly, we do not want to neglect what we have been given to oversee. We do not want to be like those who live outside of the Set-Apart Place. The dominion overseers have taken for granted their gift of being among *the living* and their Earth home. They chose not to till or work the ground of their own hearts and that has spilled over to how they now take care of the Earth. They are not digging up the barren grounds of their hearts nor are they taking care of the Earth's soil; therefore, it is starving. Furthermore, I don't even want to begin the day talking about all the wrongness they are doing to our animal friends."

"I know, my love, let's not go there this morning, let's keep it joyful."

"Yes, my love. We are set-apart and do not want to be like them. We have a special calling on our beings – to live a set-apart lifestyle while maintaining a set-apart diet. One day, when we are ripe and mature, the Master Gardener will call us to go forth out of the boundaries of the Fence-of-Fire. Then, we will get to teach the dominion overseers how beneficial it is to be obedient and follow the Instructions for Life that He has given us."

Eve paused for a minute and then responded. "I know you are right, my love. That is twice this morning."

"What is twice this morning?"

"That is twice already that I have said you are right."

"Well," Adam responded with a humorous grin.

Eve responded with love and adoration.

"Adam, I know you are right. And I know you are wise. Sometimes I just feel like I should be able to make some decisions around here."

"Of course you should, my love. And I want that too," Adam said, while drawing Eve even closer to his being.

"Then why am I treated less than?"

"Less than what, my love? I am nothing special above you. Remember, we were not created to be exactly alike. You have your gifts and talents and I have mine. It is our singularity that makes up our awesome oneness. We are different in some ways, but we do work together on all matters."

"I know that, Adam, but I don't think you are hearing what I am trying to say."

"Okay, my love, run it by me once more. What are you trying to say? I will listen more intently."

"My love, it should be obvious that I am treated less than if I cannot make any of the decisions around here."

At this point, Adam began to speak softer to Eve. He took her face and cupped it in his hands while gently drawing her even closer.

"I hear you, my love, and I agree. I think it will be great for you to make some decisions about how we spend our days. You are wise and intelligent too and deserve that opportunity. As for today, it would be disciplined for us to complete the task that is set before us. Let's knock this out of the way and then I promise this afternoon and tomorrow I will let you choose what you want to do, and we will do it."

"Oh, my love, you always make me feel good. Thank you for loving me."

Adam then began to give Eve an all-encompassing hug, lifting her feet off the floor of their tree house and spinning both of their beings around in joyful delight.

"I truly do love my female!" he shouted.

"And I truly do love my male!" she shouted back.

Eve could feel the vibration of Adam's heartbeat. She knew their beats were synchronized in a harmonious rhythm. This made her heart smile, and she was glad to be snug in his arms.

Adam and Eve were enjoying their embrace when Adam suddenly realized that the Greater Light was rising.

"Oh no," he said with concern.

"What is it, my love?"

"The Greater Light is rising, and it is time for our morning communion with the Master Gardener!"

"Oh, yes, it is! The Greater Light is rising."

Adam released Eve from his embrace and began to look around. He really did need to get going.

"Where are we meeting the Master Gardener for communion?" Eve asked.

"He wanted us to meet Him in the peppermint patch near the Tree of Life. You stay here and tidy things up. I don't think the Master Gardener will mind if I represent us both. Besides, you still have sleepiness in your eyes."

"Well, you'd better hurry off then. He will be concerned about us if we do not keep His second most important instruction."

Adam agreed with Eve.

"Okay, I am going to run make that appointment. I don't think I will be long, but I am not for certain. Since you are staying back, just prepare to meet me in the carrot and turnip patches."

"Sure, my love, I will do that."

Heading toward the exit of their tree house, Adam stopped in his tracks. He then turned and walked over to a corner where a large basket that held various tools sat.

"I'd better grab my handy-dandy wonderful wooden garden tool. This sure does make turning the soil over easier. And, my love, will you also please remember to bring our gourd cups when you come? We can use them while drinking from the spring today, on our break."

"Yes, I will bring them."

"And what about packing some of those walnuts and pecans – the ones we gathered yesterday? Those will make for a great snack."

"Sure, I will do that too."

"Oh! And one more thing."

"Adam, you have got to get going."

"Will you please grab two peaches from the peach trees, while you are on your way to meet me in the patches? I have really been wanting a fresh peach."

"Yes, my love. I have you covered. I will gather the cups, nuts, and peaches along the way and meet you soon. Now, go! You do not want to cause the Master Gardener to be concerned."

"Thanks, my love. Okay, I am off. See you shortly in the carrot and turnip patches."

Kissing Eve on the forehead, Adam waved goodbye and moved towards the exit of their tree house. Eve watched as he climbed down their ladder. With joy in her heart, she thought, *My little tree monkey*.

CHAPTER TWELVE

INDEPENDENT EVE

O kay, I have our cups, walnuts, and pecans. Now, to head toward the carrot and turnip patches, picking up two peaches along the way, Eve thought to herself, as she caught a glimpse of a beautiful rabbit standing near the path she was heading toward.

"Yes, I know, I know, rabbit. I am headed to get those patches ready for you. Thanks for the reminder!"

The Master Gardener had caused a wise rabbit to cross Eve's path. He used this encounter to remind Eve of her destination.

The carrot and turnip patches are not that far away. If I hurry, I can make it there and start turning over the soil before my love even gets there. He will be so impressed. But wait – even though Adam said the appointment might not take that long, I probably still have a little time to spare before they finish. The peppermint patch is a good distance away from the carrot and turnip patches, so it will take Adam a bit of time to walk over once he and the Master Gardener are finished. So maybe I could throw in a quick exploring excursion after all. It wouldn't take long to run out to the area I have been wanting to explore and then get back to the patches.

Eve had talked herself into something she should not have been doing. Adam had told her to meet him at the carrot and turnip patches, and reaching that destination should have been her priority.

CHAPTER THIRTEEN

MEETING WITH THE MASTER GARDENER

"**S**halom, Master Gardener!" Adam said as he ran up to embrace his Maker.

"Well, shalom, My child! Hold on, hold on! First, take a deep breath. Now, calm down. Are you okay?"

"Yes!" exclaimed Adam, "I am okay."

"Is Eve okay?"

"Yes, Master Gardener, she is okay."

"Good. For a minute there I wondered why she was not with you. You are out of breath and have been running fast. I am glad to hear all is well, though. Now, fill me in on what your hurry is all about."

"Yes, Master Gardener. I did not want to cause You concern by being late to our morning appointment. I know I can run faster than Eve, therefore I told her I would represent us both and she could stay back, tidy things up, and prepare to meet me in the carrot and turnip patches once our communion was over."

"I see. Well, now that you are here, and you have caught your breath, give me that big hug you were about to run me over with!"

Adam stepped towards the Master Gardener and the Master Gardener stepped towards him. They embraced in a brief and loving hug.

"I am glad you made it this morning, Adam. I believe it's time you and Eve learned how to test the nutrient levels of the soil in this beautiful and set-apart place. You mentioned the carrot and turnip patches. Is that your chore for today?"

"Wow, that sounds interesting, Master Gardener. And yes, that is our chore for today. I have plans for us to work the soil and get it ready for a new planting. After that, I told Eve I would take her exploring. But if you have something else in mind, I can change our plans."

"Well, it is best that you get the soil for those patches ready for a new planting. That is important. How about you and Eve continue with your plans, and then when you are finished, come find Me. I will be working near here, just a couple of patches over in the marigold meadow."

"Sure, Master Gardener, that sounds awesome!"

"We can then start testing the nutrient levels in the soil at a couple of places throughout this beautiful and sacred place. I even know just the area I would like to show our Eve, one with beautiful trees having flowers that smell heavenly and limbs that are stair-stepped. I know she will like that," the Master Gardener said.

"She sure will. That is very kind of You, Master Gardener. She does like to explore, and she loves interesting trees."

"Yes, she does, My son."

"Amazing. That sounds great, Master Gardener! We will look forward to learning more about the soil and how to keep it healthy, and Eve will be really excited about the new spot for exploring you are going to show us."

"Great!" the Master Gardener said.

"Yes, we will be there! It shouldn't take us long in the patches. We will get it done in no time, especially now that we have something really neat to look forward to."

"Wonderful. I am delighted and well-pleased! Now you run along, and you and Eve get those patches turned over. I will see you when you are done."

"Yes, Master Gardener, we will see you soon," Adam responded.

As Adam began to turn to leave the peppermint patch, something within his being stopped him.

I can't leave just yet. I really want to know. I pray He doesn't get upset with me for asking, but this has been stirring within my being for several days now and I feel like I am going to explode.

"What is it, Son? Are you okay?"

"Yes, Master Gardener, I am well."

Adam's voice was cracking from his nervousness. He felt unsettled and excited all at the same time.

Why am I shaking inside?

"Son, whatever it is, just know that you can always come to Me. I am here for you."

Adam trusted the Master Gardener more than he trusted himself.

I am going for it. I am going to ask Him.

Trembling and yet determined, Adam was able to muster up his confidence. And, although he was nervous, he also knew that his Maker was trustworthy.

"Master Gardener, I have something on my mind and in my heart."

"I am listening. You know I love you."

"Well, Master Gardener, thank You for being willing to teach us so many awesome things, just like teaching us about the nutrients in the soil. Learning about the soil in this set-apart place is something Eve and I both need to know about, so we can grow in knowledge and understanding of how to keep it as beautiful as you have designed it to be."

"Yes, Adam, that is my intent, but also to teach you both how to govern this place in right-ruling."

"Thank you for creating us, Master Gardener, and thank you for creating this sacred place for us to reside in."

"You are welcome, My son. I am glad we are in this together, and I look forward to all the wonderful things that will become of you and your little ray of sunshine."

"Oh, Master Gardener, You are the best! I love you so much!"

"I love you more, Adam."

Being moved by Adam's love, the Master Gardener gave him another brief hug. He could sense that Adam needed to get some things off his mind and wanted to create a safe place for him to feel comfortable doing that.

"Master Gardener?"

"Yes, Adam?"

"I just have one thing to ask You before I head out."

"I am listening, My child. Go ahead and tell me what is on your mind. You will feel better for doing so."

"Yes, Master Gardener. I was just wondering ... um ... I mean ... um, okay, here goes: When will you teach Eve and I about being fruitful and multiplying?"

Why did I fumble at my words? Why am I so nervous?

The Master Gardener's countenance showed that He welcomed Adam's question.

Oh, good! I don't think He is bothered that I asked.

"My child, even before now, I have been sensing your desire to talk about this."

"You have?"

"Yes."

"So, it is okay that I asked?"

"Of course! You should always feel free to ask Me anything. And yes, we will be talking about this in the coming days. I do believe you and Eve are maturing at a rate that very soon you will be multiplying."

Yes!

"Let's first get you up to date on how to test the soil, and then we will choose a day when we can discuss what it means to have a joined embrace."

"Joined embrace?"

"Yes, joined embrace. It is what activates your fruitfulness, making it possible for you two to multiply."

Adam looked a little confused.

"Don't you worry, I will explain all you need to know."

"I know you will, Master Gardener. I trust you!"

"Now you run along and get those chores done. I will see you and Eve when you are finished."

"Thank you, Master Gardener! You are the best!"

"I love you, Son!"

Chapter Fourteen

THE ERROR OF EVE

While Adam was meeting with the Master Gardener, Eve had decided to wander off from the path that would have carried her straight to the carrot and turnip patches. She justified it in her mind that it was okay.

"What harm am I doing, anyway? Everyone needs an adventure, right, little deer?"

A wise male deer stood in the middle of Eve's path. And although she addressed him as being "little," he was nowhere near that. This male deer was grand and majestic, carrying twelve points on his broad set of antlers.

"Do you speak, deer? Or are you just going to stand there and stare right through me?" she asked.

This wasn't the first deer that Eve had come across that morning – a female also had tried to deter her. The deer were trying to send her a message, but Eve's desire to wander off was greater and she wasn't hearing them.

"Move over, deer. Share the path!"

The wise male deer didn't budge. He just stood still, looking at Eve for an answer as to why she was exploring so far from her and Adam's tree house, all alone.

"Everyone needs some alone time, deer, even you. Now please move aside so I can continue my excursion."

The wise male deer still didn't budge.

"Fine, I will go around."

Eve had to move some tall bushes and branches of smaller trees out of her way, but she finally managed to move past him. And once she passed her roadblock, she didn't look back.

What's the big deal, anyway? I am a big girl. What does it matter if I explore all by myself? It's not like I am hurting anyone. And I still have plenty of time before Adam will be back at the carrot and turnip patches.

Every step Eve took past the wise deer drew her farther away from the carrot and turnip patches. And with every step she took, she gained a newfound confidence in herself.

Hmm, I wonder what is over there? she thought.

Eve looked off into the distance. She had spotted an area she had never explored before. It was a forest filled with all sorts of beautiful species of bushes, trees, and vines. There were even a few large magnolia trees spread out and growing throughout the area.

Ah, magnolia trees! Their flowers are so big and beautiful, I want to go there.

Eve could tell that the area she wanted to explore was very close to the Fence-of-Fire. This would not have been a big deal, except both the Master Gardener and Adam had warned her not to get too close to it.

What is "too close to it," anyway? They did not specify that. How am I really supposed to know?

Eve continued to move toward the area.

I am going to do it. That's it. That is where I will go. I have been wanting to familiarize myself with the magnolia trees for a while and now seems like the perfect time to do it. The Master Gardener says the bark of the tree is beneficial for us, if steeped as a tea, and the aroma of its flower petals is good for our moods, whatever that means. And I have just a little time before I need to turn back. Wait! Oh no, I still haven't picked the peaches Adam asked me to bring! Oh well, I will just have to hurry.

Picking up her pace, Eve made her way through the thick forest area of vines, bushes, and trees. Becoming more determined with every step, she spotted a tree she wanted to climb.

There it is. The most beautiful magnolia tree I have ever seen.

Eve stood there for a long minute before her excitement began to fade. The tree that she wanted to climb was very close to the Fence-of-Fire, and from her observation – the closest.

I have seen the Fence-of-Fire before – several times, actually. I know, I know, always from a distance, but what is the big deal, anyway? The Master Gardener and Adam both warned me about it, but that's because it is a boundary, and they were just concerned that I might want to cross it. I don't want to cross it. I just want to enjoy climbing the tree that is growing near it. Look at how large and impressive it is.

The magnolia tree grew in such a fashion that its lower branches almost touched the soil. For Eve, it looked like stair steps, only in the form of sturdy branches.

I can climb this tree in no time. Then, I will head back to the path that the peach trees are on, and that path will bring me nearer to the carrot and turnip patches. I will beat Adam there for sure.

Chapter Fifteen

ADAM IS GLOWING

Adam's light beamed bright. He had deep gratitude for his Maker and loved being in His presence.

He is so good to me! I love Him so much!

The Master Gardener's words had hit Adam in the core of his being, and he now loved Him even more than he did the day before.

Wow! Soon Eve and I will be about our Maker's business! Soon we will be fruitful and multiplying! I am so delighted, and I know Eve will be too!

As Adam scurried off to meet Eve, thoughts raced through his being.

Hmm, I wonder how long it's going to take me to get to the carrot and turnip patches? I am really excited to tell Eve we are going to learn how to test the nutrient levels within the soil. But more than that, I cannot wait to tell her that we are mature enough to learn how to be fruitful and multiply our union! Now, I have to pick up the pace and go meet my Eve!

CHAPTER SIXTEEN

ACCESS IS GRANTED

E ve climbed as far as she could up the magnolia tree. Now she needed to turn and climb back down. She would have loved to have stayed longer, but she had told Adam she would meet him.

Why couldn't he just let me go exploring first? Then we could have spent the rest of the day working the patches. This is such a beautiful view! Oh, I love it!

Eve stopped for a moment before she began her descent. Breathing in the beautiful scenery, her eyes scanned the horizon, far and wide.

Ah, it's magnificent – the sights, the sounds, the beautiful and breathtaking view!

Several minutes passed before Eve realized that she had probably stayed there a little longer than she had anticipated.

Okay, it is time to go. It is time to make my way down. Maybe I will bring Adam back here this afternoon. I think he will really like this tree and the scenery that is all around. He will be thankful that I found such a beautiful view. I know he loves those too.

Oh, wait! I cannot tell him about this place. I cannot tell him I came here. He would want to ask me how I found it and I would have to tell him what I did. I will just keep it to myself for now. I don't want to run the risk of him being upset with me.

Eve glanced down at the tree limbs below her. She did not realize she had climbed so far from the ground. She had not been nervous climbing up the tree, but now, she felt an extreme uneasiness concerning the amount of distance that was between her and the soil.

I am okay. I am fine. There is plenty of tree here, plenty of branches. I am not going to fall. I will not look down too far.

Eve continued to talk to herself, trying to coerce herself into confidence, but it was not working. Her heart pounded heavily, and her being began to sweat. Startled by her own fear of falling, she became debilitated, trapped, and unable to move.

Focus, Eve, just focus on making slow movements and making your way down.

Eve's feet were firmly situated on the limb below her. One of her arms was wrapped around the trunk of the tree, while her other arm and hand gripped a branch that ran just above her head. There were several branches all around her and below. She was, by all appearances, safe, but by no means did she feel that way. She felt very unsteady and was trembling inside.

Why is my light dimming?

As panic began to take over, Eve's eyes caught a glimpse of an unfamiliar but very beautiful being standing near but just outside the Fence-of-Fire.

Oh my, something is watching me! How long has it been there? And, why is it living outside of the most beautiful place in all the Earth?

Eve was not only surprised by the presence of the being, she was also mesmerized by its appearance. At first glance she thought it to be male, being tall, strong, handsome, and having features like her male Adam. But, on a second look, she thought it might be female, for it carried an elegance in its movements. Instead of having an inner light that shined outwardly, like her and Adam, this being lit up from its luminous covering, which was patterned in a glossy mosaic design that transitioned back and forth from being vibrantly colored one minute to dull and soft tones the next.

"Shalom, dear one," the beautiful being said.

It is talking to me!

Eve did not know what to say. She did not know how to respond. She had never spoken to anyone outside of the Fence-of-Fire. She continued to hold on to the tree's trunk and the branch right above her head. Her grip grew tighter and tighter, causing the tips of her fingers to turn blue. She did not know how long she could last this way. Her mind was racing.

Oh, Eve! Why did you get yourself into this situation? If only I had respected Adam and went directly to where I told him I would be! What am I going to do now? How can I get myself down? I feel so frozen. I am paralyzed with fear, and my light is growing dim. My heart is racing, and my head is spinning.

The beautiful being could see Eve panicking and decided to speak up.

"Looksss like you have gotten yourssself into a tricky predicament. May I be of any ssservice to you, dear one?"

Eve was now frightened and did not know what to do.

"I am not sure how you can help. I am over here, and you are over there."

"Oh, I can help you, dear one! I am very trained in climbing up and down treesss. All you have to do is invite me in. Then I can crosss this fence and come to your aid. I can have you feeling sssafe again in no time."

Although Eve's mind was racing in a million directions, she was also thinking upon the beautiful being's offer.

Maybe it wouldn't hurt to invite the being in here. I know this place is set-apart, but I am in need. I need help, and I need it now!

Eve decided to converse further with the being, for not only was she intrigued by it, but talking to it also helped deflect her from her fear of falling. And she judged it as being kind, intelligent, and having a willingness to help.

"I do not even know what kind of being you are, nor your name," she said.

"It'sss okay, friend. I am a ssself-serpent, and you can call me sssso. And what is your name, dear?"

"My name is Eve. I have never known of a self-serpent before. What are you doing around here?"

"Ah, my new friend, I am glad you asked! Ssself-serpents are known for helping othersss learn how to ssserve themselvesss. And I was just minding my own businesss over here when I happened to look up and sssee you high in a tree, but ssstruggling to get the courage to climb down."

"How did you know?"

"Ah, it's my job to know. I am actually pretty good at watching out for othersss who need a little help. You don't know thisss yet, but the name 'ssself-serpent' is associated with ssserving 'ssself.' And because ssself-serpentsss know how to help and ssserve their own ssselves, they also can help othersss do the same. For example, thisss sssituation that I have happened upon – you being ssstuck in thisss tree. I know it is making you uneasy, but I also know I can take that uneasinesss away from you. Dear friend, if you would like to be rescued from thisss sssituation, I can help you learn how to ssserve yourssself by coaching you down this tree."

Because panic had begun to take over, and she was not thinking soberly, Eve decided to take the self-serpent up on its offer. Inviting it into the Set-Apart Place, she watched with wonderment as it walked right through the Fence-of-Fire.

It didn't get burned! she thought.

After the self-serpent was inside the Set-Apart Place it began to make its way over to the base of the magnolia tree. Stopping briefly, it looked up at Eve and gave her a reassuring smile. "You will be jussst fine. I will have you down in no time."

Being thankful that she would soon be rescued, Eve responded, "Thank you, Self-serpent. You are extremely kind."

"My pleasure," said the self-serpent.

Eve's anxiety began to lessen, for the help she requested was at hand. She watched as the self-serpent slithered up the magnolia tree. Once it arrived, her inquisitiveness took precedence.

"How did you do that?"

"How did I do what?" the self-serpent replied.

"Climb this tree, in the way that you did? You have limbs like my male and I do, yet you slithered up this tree so effortlessly?"

"Well, my dear, we all have our giftsss and talentsss. For the time being, let'sss focusss on getting you down from here."

"Yes, Self-serpent. I agree, that is the priority."

***

"I told you I would have you feeling sssafe in no time."

"Thank you, Self-serpent. I did not know what I was going to do. I did not know how I was going to climb down this tree. Thank you for being here for me. Thank you for your help. It was very kind of you."

"It was my pleasure, friend."

I have got to get out of here. I need to get going. This being is so different, beautifully different. I am intrigued. I wish I could stay longer, but I really do need to get going.

Eve was looking around as if she needed to hurry off, and truly she did need to. She needed to get back to Adam. She needed to get back to the carrot and turnip patches as quickly as she could.

"Okay, well, um … I need to get back to my chores. Can you see yourself back over the fence, Self-serpent?"

"Of courssse I can. You run along and take care of what you need to take care of."

"I am really sorry I have to run off, but I do need to get going."

"I will be fine! Go," the self-serpent said in a reassuring voice.

In her time of distress, Eve had invited the self-serpent into the most set-apart place in all the Earth. Now, she was trusting that it would see its way out. But would it?

Chapter Seventeen

Great and Greater News

E ve ran as fast as she could. She tried to get to the patches before Adam arrived, but she was too late. He was already there, down on his knees, turning over the soil with his favorite wooden tool.

"Hello, my love! I was starting to get concerned. Are you okay?"

Eve was out of breath and filled with much anxiety.

What am I going to tell him? What excuse can I give? What is this stirring in my being? Why do I feel this way? Ugh.

Adam began to be concerned that something might be wrong, so he stopped what he was doing and stood up. He stared at Eve, as if telling her he was ready for her response.

"I got distracted."

"Distracted? When? When I left you at our tree house, or on your way over here?"

"On my way over here. You know how I get, Adam."

"No, I don't know how you get, Eve. Please explain."

"You know how I get to thinking about something and before long, my pace slows. It just took me a while to get here because I got distracted in my thoughts and that really slowed me down."

"From my observation, your pace was not slow at all. You were running full steam ahead when you arrived. And you were out of breath."

Adam was not upset with Eve, but she took it that way. And instead of being thankful that he was concerned about her welfare, evident through his inquisitiveness, she became frustrated and short with him.

"So what, Adam? When I realized I was lagging, I thought to myself about how upset you would be at me for being late, then I started running to get here. I tried to beat you here, but I didn't make it. Are you satisfied? Do you have your answers now?"

"No, I am not satisfied, Eve. And where is this attitude coming from? I have never gotten upset with you, so I don't know why you would think that. I was just concerned – that's all!"

"I don't want to talk about it anymore, Adam. Let's just drop it."

"Fine. Help me get this soil turned over."

Adam continued to work the soil. Eve joined in but kept her distance and stayed quiet. This caused Adam to feel drained and tired. He did not understand what was wrong with his other half, for up until that day, Eve had always been uplifting and encouraging.

After finishing their chore, Adam chose to break the silence.

"Ah, good – we are done. And it is time for a snack. How about some walnuts and pecans and one of those juicy peaches you picked for us."

Eve was caught off guard. She had totally forgotten all about the peaches.

What could be my excuse? she thought.

Adam realized there was still something wrong with his Eve. He did not want to argue with her, but to love her.

"What is wrong, my love?"

"I forgot about the peaches."

"Forgot?"

"Yes, I forgot them, Adam!" she snapped.

"Okay, okay, Eve. You forgot them. What is bugging you? Why are you being this way? This is not my Eve."

"I do not want to talk about it, Adam. Just drop it."

"Okay, Eve, I will drop it," he said, resigned. "Let's talk about something else."

Eve continued to be silent for several minutes, while mixed emotions swirled within Adam's being. He was so joyful after his appointment with the Master Gardener, but now he was struggling against feelings of confusion concerning Eve's attitude. But even so, he was determined to bring up the subject that he had been looking forward to sharing with her.

"Hey, I've got some great news, my love, and even some greater news!"

Eve hesitated but then decided to respond.

"What is it, Adam? What is your great and greater news?"

"Well, the great news is that the Master Gardener is going to teach us how to test the nutrient levels within the soil of this place."

"Why do we need to know how to do that?"

"I do not know, but I am sure there is a good reason, and we will find out."

"That does not sound like that great of news to me."

What is wrong with her?! Adam thought to himself.

He could not believe the change in his mate, for she was not the same as when he had left her that morning.

"And the greater news, Eve, is that once we learn about that, He is then going to teach us how to be fruitful and multiply our union!"

"Is that all your meeting was about?"

Ugh! She's not even excited.

"Yes, well, at least the great news was. But I am the one who brought up the subject of being fruitful and multiplying, when I was leaving. And I thought it was greater news. I really thought you would be excited, Eve. It won't be long, and we will know how to. He wants to meet with both of us this afternoon, but that will be about testing the soil. I am not sure yet when He will teach us about the joined embrace."

"Joined embrace?" Eve asked.

"Yes, that is what the Master Gardener called it. The way I understood it is that the joined embrace would bring forth our fruit and multiply our union from our own seed. Isn't that awesome, my love! Aren't you excited?"

"But I thought we were going exploring this afternoon."

"Yes, Eve, we still are. We are just going to do it with the Master Gardener. He said He would take us to a few different places to test the nutrient levels within the soil and then He would show us some new areas to explore."

Eve was not sure if this was great news or not. And she did not allow herself to even start to think about the greater news Adam was talking about. She was very hesitant in her joy and quite nervous with the thought of having to be around the Master Gardener. She already felt such guilt knowing that she was keeping something from Adam, and she was not sure how long she could hide it from him. Being around the Master Gardener would only make matters worse, for she knew He was all-knowing and wise.

CHAPTER EIGHTEEN

AN AFTERNOON WITH THE MASTER GARDENER

E ve reluctantly went along with Adam to meet the Master Gardener. They found Him right where He said He would be, in the marigold meadow near the Tree of Life. After a few minutes in His presence, Eve's anxiety ceased, and she was able to experience shalom.

If the Master Gardener knows what I did, He sure isn't letting on.

There were several areas within the Set-Apart Place that Adam and Eve had yet to discover. As they followed the Master Gardener away from the meadow, both could not help but wonder where He might be taking them.

"Eve! Pay attention. You're lagging and slowing us down," Adam said.

"Ah, there it is," the Master Gardener said. "This is the way that leads to the perfect spot to begin testing the nutrients in the soil. Follow Me. We are almost there."

Eve rolled her eyes at Adam. And although He didn't say anything, she soon realized the Master Gardener had seen her do it. This caused her to feel shame, and her light began to dim again.

"Why do you always have to make me look bad in front of Him?" Eve whispered to Adam as they continued to follow the Master Gardener.

"Why do you speak in absolutes, Eve? You know I don't 'always' make you look bad in front of the Master Gardener. You are making things up in your head."

"Did you have to bring it to His attention that I was lagging?"

"I didn't have to bring anything to His attention, Eve. What makes you think He didn't notice to begin with? You underestimate Him."

Eve gave Adam another eye roll, and this time she didn't even care if the Master Gardener saw or not.

CHAPTER NINETEEN

EVE HIDES HER SECRET

E ve's heart began to race, and she felt as if her stomach was turning over. The Master Gardener had led them to the forest that she had explored all by herself earlier. And as they continued to follow Him, she soon realized they were heading right to the very tree that she had climbed.

"Here we are. Isn't it a beautiful place? Isn't this a beautiful tree?" the Master Gardener asked.

"Wow! Yes, Master Gardener, this is a beautiful place, and a beautiful tree," Adam responded, in awe of the sight.

At this point, Eve was frozen in her tracks. Although she was trying to conceal her anxiety, she wasn't doing a very good job of it. That alone caused her anxiety to increase.

Do they know? Can they see how nervous I am?

Both Adam and the Master Gardener looked her way, waiting for her response. She didn't know what to say. They were both smiling at her, which only made her more anxious.

Get it together, Eve! Come to your senses, she thought.

"Yes, Master Gardener, this is a beautiful place, and it is a beautiful tree," she managed to say.

"Ah, I knew you would like it. I was even thinking of you when I picked out this location. I know how you like to explore. After I show you and Adam how to test the soil here, maybe you would like to climb this tree with Me?"

Eve's stomach began to tighten, and her pulse began to race.

"That tree looks really tall. Maybe I shouldn't climb such a tall tree. What if I get up there and become afraid to climb back down?"

"Afraid?" Adam asked.

Eve responded in agitation.

"Yes, Adam, afraid."

"I have never heard of such a thing," he said, with a confused expression on his face.

"I know it is a tall tree, My daughter. I have already thought about that," the Master Gardener said.

Adam was confused. He didn't know why Eve was acting like this.

"That is why I wanted to climb it with you and be by your side, My child."

"That is very kind of you, Master Gardener," Adam softly interjected.

The Master Gardener gently extended His arm out towards Eve. Touching her on the shoulder He continued to speak.

"I know what you speak of when you mention 'fear.' It can be debilitating. But as long as we are together, I can help you face any obstacle of fear you may encounter. And not only that, but I can help you overcome it, causing you to no longer be plagued by it."

At this point the Master Gardener looked at Adam and said, "Come closer, My son."

Reaching out to touch him on his shoulder too, the Master Gardener told Adam to grab a hold of Eve's hand. Then, He continued to lovingly teach them both.

"Fear is a liar, and My children should never have to face it alone. Together, we will overthrow it and destroy the works of darkness for good."

Eve's eyes swelled with tears while Adam simply stared at the Master Gardener. He was amazed at the wisdom that flowed out of His mouth.

Eve became very quiet, and this perturbed Adam even more, to the point that he gave her a very stern look.

What is she thinking?

He lowered his voice and began to whisper her way.

"The Master Gardener had you in mind when thinking of this place, Eve. The least you can do is respond in gratitude."

Eve decided she needed to speak up, but her head was spinning, for she was determined to keep her secret hidden.

"Thank you for thinking of me, Master Gardener," she said, with a reluctant grin.

Frustration was now overtaking Adam's calm demeanor.

"Eve! What is wrong with you?"

Eve quieted again. Adam thought she was ignoring him, but she was just distracted and in shock by what her eyes were beholding. Adam could not see it because he was facing Eve, but on the other side of him, several yards away, stood a beautiful being slightly hidden behind a tree. And this was not just any beautiful being – this was the self-serpent who Eve had invited into the Set-Apart Place earlier that morning. This was the self-serpent that had crossed the Fence-of-Fire and helped her in her time of need. This was the self-serpent that was supposed to have seen its way out but obviously had not.

Eve's mind raced.

Ugh, Self-serpent! Why didn't you see yourself out? What are you still doing here? Does the Master Gardener see it? Does he know? I know Adam cannot see it, but oh my, what am I going to do?

Eve was quiet for the rest of the afternoon. After they finished learning how to test the nutrients of the soil under the magnolia tree, she declined to climb the tree with the Master Gardener, and they all moved on to another location, eventually ending up back where they had started.

Eve had really annoyed Adam that day, but what could he do? He had no idea what was causing her to be so distant and when he tried to speak to her, it only made matters worse.

The Master Gardener took it all in stride. He did not let Eve's demeanor rob him of His joy, and He was not deterred from reaching His goals for the day. He continued in shalom, teaching both Adam and Eve how to test the soil at various locations throughout the Set-Apart Place.

Chapter Twenty

BETWEEN TWO TREES

After they returned to the marigold meadow, the Master Gardener told Adam and Eve He wanted to share one more instruction with them before they called it a day.

"Yes, Master Gardener!" Adam responded with kindness. He thought the Master Gardener was going to bring up the subject of joined embrace.

Eve just stood there. She was so ready to get away from the Master Gardener and Adam. She wanted to be finished with the day so she could process the events and figure out what she needed to do concerning the self-serpent who had obviously never seen its way out of the Set-Apart Place.

"Today you learned a lot about testing the soil, but there is still a very important rule that you will need to know," the Master Gardener said.

Eve's ears perked up. Although she was ready to leave, she was also intrigued.

"No amount of testing the soil will ever change it. But it can be changed over time, as one takes the time to nurture it, by putting what is good into it. This simple truth and rule to follow, of putting good into the soil, can change the soil's productivity for the rest of its life. Therefore, I am giving you good instructions when I tell you to only put 'good' into the soil of the Earth. Likewise, I am giving you good instructions when I tell you to only put 'good' into the soil of your beings."

Adam and Eve both nodded and verbally agreed with the Master Gardener.

"Now, I have placed two trees within this Set-Apart Place – two trees that are very important for you to know about."

"Yes, Master Gardener, we are standing between those two trees," Adam said, while Eve again nodded her head in acknowledgment.

"Yes, My beloveds, you are. You are standing between those two trees. And while one is called the Tree of Life and pertains to it, the other is called the Tree of the Knowledge of Good and Evil and does not pertain to life but rather to death."

The Master Gardener paused for a moment. He knew Eve had questions.

"Eve, would you like to ask something?"

She hesitated.

"Go ahead and ask your question, Eve. He's given you permission," Adam said.

"Well, Master Gardener, I was just wondering why the Tree of the Knowledge of Good and Evil pertains to death. How can something pertain to death if it has good in it?"

"I am glad you asked that question, Eve, for there is a simple answer. If you and Adam adhere to this understanding, it will save you a lot of time and much heartache."

Time, heartache ... What is He truly speaking of? Adam thought.

"When you mix what is good with what is evil, the good becomes tainted. It is no longer pure. It is no longer lovely. It becomes clouded over with a veil of darkness, and although the good may struggle to continue to shine brightly, it cannot. This is because its authority over the evil has been denied, through the allowance of the mixing.

"On the other hand, when evil is not allowed to be mixed with good, then that is when victory and beauty will sprout forth. Do you remember our discussions about the dominion overseers, and how they had the opportunity to destroy evil but instead they began to mix with it?"

"I remember," Adam said.

Then both the Master Gardener and Adam turned towards Eve, to wait for her response. After a long pause, she finally spoke up and answered.

"Yes, Master Gardener, I remember."

"That is what I am talking about here. The dominion overseers were supposed to overcome evil by not mixing with it, but because they did, they have lost any right to live eternally. Choosing to partake in only what is good grants one access to the right of eternal life. Choosing to mix that good with evil causes that right to be void.

"Out of the Tree of Life, every 'good' tree, plant, vine, and patch of soil is nurtured. Even you, My children. And out of the Tree of the Knowledge of Good and Evil comes only heartache and destruction. These you were not made for. You were made set-apart to grow in all knowledge of good, wisdom, discipline, kindness, and compassion. And, one day, having grown in these attributes, you will teach the dominion overseers how to repent, by denying all mixing and returning to only what is good. Therefore, hear Me out and be very mindful of what I am saying, for I do not want you to be deceived. You were made for everything good that pertains to life. The Tree of the Knowledge of Good and Evil will not sustain you. And, if it were to be given your time and attention, you would then be feeding it the very power it needs to destroy you.

"You are encouraged to partake in the Tree of Life, and all the other species of plants, vines, and trees that its fountain of waters nourish. Do this as often as you like. This tree supplies you with My table of food that is prepared for you, your health, and your well-being. But of the Tree of the Knowledge of Good and Evil, you are not to partake. You are not to nurture its soil, nor are you to eat its fruit. Its bounty is sweet to the eyes and tasty on the tongue, but its outcome is bitterness to the belly, destroying the mind, the heart, and the bowels. Stay away from the Tree of the Knowledge of Good and Evil. It was not prepared for you, My beloved and set-apart children. Stay away."

CHAPTER TWENTY-ONE

THE CUNNING SELF-SERPENT

The self-serpent had followed the three back to the marigold meadow. It lurked nearby and listened in as the Master Gardener instructed Adam and Eve to stay away from the Tree of the Knowledge of Good and Evil. This only made the self-serpent more curious, and because of its deviant nature, it decided to make the tree its new hideout.

Spiraling up and down its trunk and throughout its branches, the self-serpent began to familiarize itself with the Tree of the Knowledge of Good and Evil. And, as it continued to study the tree, it wondered why this tree had been marked as not being good enough for the Master Gardener's table.

Why is thisss tree marked for decay? And why should another tree be marked for life and get to live, while thisss tree is neglected? That does not sssound fair. That does not sssound right.

The self-serpent compared the Tree of the Knowledge of Good and Evil with all the other trees in the Set-Apart Place. It observed that this tree bore leaves and fruit just like the others.

Although its fruit is sssparse, it looks deliciousss, and good for food.

Noticing that the fruit and leaves looked very tasty, but were also lacking in productivity, the self-serpent came to its conclusion:

Ah, the Tree of the Knowledge of Good and Evil, in all appearance is withering, withering from a lack of attention, and most importantly from a lack of consumption. Thisss tree has been neglected, and I must do something about it!

In that moment, the self-serpent grew angry and spiteful toward the Master Gardener.

I do not like that Adam and Eve have been instructed to ssstay away from my new hideout. Thisss tree hasss gotten a bad rap and there is no reason why it shouldn't be nourished too, by the watersss that flow from the Tree of Life. If I can get thisss tree to bounce back from itsss withering state, then it will be sssaved. And once I rescue it, I will be praisssed for my good deed!

Although I must deceive Adam and Eve to accomplish my goal, they will thank me later. They will realize that it wasss far more important that they sssave thisss tree than to obey the voice of the Master Gardener. What does the Master Gardener know anyway that I don't? And who does He think He is? Why should the Master Gardener get all the praissse and esteem from His creation when He hasss neglected the Tree of the Knowledge of Good and Evil?

Once the decision had been made, a plan was underway. The cunning self-serpent contemplated what would be the best way to deceive Adam and Eve into eating the fruit from the Tree of the Knowledge of Good and Evil.

Thisss is what I must do: I will begin with Eve, and play on her emotionsss, while luring her to the path that the Tree of the Knowledge of Good and Evil is on. She will want to ssave the tree because I will convince her it is the 'good' thing to do.

The self-serpent consumed its time by stalking Eve.

Ah, my dear Eve is all alone. She is getting good at adventuring without Adam.

Once the opportunity arose to get her attention, it took advantage of the moment.

"Thisss way."

Little did the self-serpent know that Eve too was desiring to converse with it, although for different reasons. At this point she thought herself to be wise, and she was determined to cover up her decision to let it into the Set-Apart Place.

Great! Here's my opportunity to see what I can do about getting this self-serpent out of here.

"My friend, follow me thisss way."

Follow this way?

Eve's mind began to race. Her thoughts moved back and forth concerning what she should do.

Maybe I need to leave it alone, or maybe not. I don't even know if I want to deal with it right now. But wait! I have to deal with it right now. If I can get it to cross back over the Fence-of-Fire, no one will ever have to know that I let it in.

After staying quiet for a long minute, Eve decided to hear the self-serpent out.

"What's up, Self-serpent? Why and where are you wanting me to follow you?"

"Yesss. Thank you, dear one, thank you for your time. I really appreciate it. I have a puzzle to sssolve, a riddle to figure out."

"What are you talking about, Self-serpent? You are not making any sense."

"Well, that is because I have a problem, and I need your help."

"What? You, the great self-serpent that helps others, are you now in need of others to help you?"

"Um, well, Eve, my dear friend, yesss. Now let usss stay on track. You must be getting distracted by my beauty. Let usss get back to the point. I know I told you I would sssee myself out of thisss place, but Eve ..."

"Just spit it out, Self-serpent! Just tell me what you are trying to say."

"Yesss, my dear, I will get right to the point, as you request. After I helped you get sssafely down from the magnolia tree, I told you I would sssee myself out of thisss place."

"You sure did, Self-serpent, you sure did."

"But Eve, it is a very good thing that I hesitated, because when I decided to take a look around to sssee if there were othersss in need of help, I came acrosss a tree that is in dire need of sssaving. It truly does need usss to help it, Eve."

Eve gave the self-serpent an eye roll and began to turn to leave.

"Eve, please! Thisss tree needs your attention, and it needsss it quickly! I know you are compassionate, and that is why I thought you would want to know. And furthermore, I alssso believe that you would care enough to do sssomething about it."

"Self-serpent, I asked you to see yourself out of here. You told me that you would, and then you did not. Now, you are nothing more than a thorn in my side. Why should I listen to anything you have to say? Why should I help you at all?"

"You mean, help me in return," it responded.

"No, I do not mean help you in return. Why are you trying to put those words in my mouth?"

"Well, maybe it is because when you help someone out, you asssume they would return the favor sssomeday. But I guesss that'sss not how you are, Eve. I guesss I was mistaken."

Eve paused and began to think more intensely about what the self-serpent was saying. And while she paused, it knew she was considering whether to hear more or not.

"Eve, my dear, I know you will want to hear me out. I am ssstanding before you for a good reason, a very good reassson indeed. Our pathsss have crosssed because we were destined to meet and change thingsss for the better."

"Change what things for the better? Looks pretty good around here to me."

"If you will come and follow me, I will explain everything."

Eve thought for a minute and wondered if she should get back to Adam, but she could not let go of the desire to hear more. Therefore, she decided to listen to, and to follow the self-serpent, who led her straight to its hideout.

"What is that smell?" she asked as they came to an abrupt stop.

And then, all of a sudden, she knew where she was.

"Why have you brought me here, Self-serpent? The Master Gardener instructed us to stay away from this tree."

The self-serpent hissed and then responded.

"But Eve, my dear, did He really mean what He said? Or was the Master Gardener putting a tessst before you both to sssee if you had the ssstrength and determination within yourssselves to become your own master gardenersss?"

"Our own master gardeners?"

"Yesss!"

"The Master Gardener gave us strict instructions to only partake of His table of food. This tree is not of His table. We are not supposed to even touch it."

"Ah, but this tree is ssstarving for attention, Eve. Itsss leavesss are beginning to wither, and if it does not get help sssoon, itsss fruit will begin to decay. It is dying from neglect. Don't you sssee?" The self-serpent indicated the blackened tree trunk.

"That is not my fault, Self-serpent."

"This is true, Eve. You cannot be held accountable for its current ssstate, but if you and Adam do not move fassst, you will both be responsible for itsss demissse."

"What do you mean, Self-serpent? We are not responsible for this tree."

"Oh, but aren't you? Can't you sssee it crying out for help?" The self-serpent motioned toward a dark, sticky substance that was seeping from the bark. "And are you ssso far removed from just a short time ago when you yoursssself needed help? Remember getting ssstuck in the magnolia tree? Did you not receive help?"

Eve's demeanor began to soften, and the self-serpent knew it had her right where it wanted her.

"I see you and Adam partaking of all the other treesss in the Set-Apart Place, and they ssstay looking energetic and fresh."

"That is because the Master Gardener told us to. He told us that as we partake of the fruit of the trees it prunes them and prepares them to keep producing more goodness."

"And that is exactly what I am trying to get acrosss to you, my beautiful Eve."

It called me "Its beautiful."

"This is the only tree here that no one hasss partaken of, and it is not looking ssso good, Eve. If thisss tree becomesss unproductive, it most certainly will be your and Adam'sss fault. You say the Master Gardener sssaid not to touch thisss tree, but if you know that you can do good by sssaving it, and you do not, isn't that jussst like holding back compassion when you have the power to extend it? And furthermore, the third Instruction for Life is to follow the Good Way, filling the Earth with actsss of kindnesss and compassion. Eve, hear what I am sssaying to you. In thisss regard it reveals that the Master Gardener must have sssome double-mindednesss, for it is not right to let thisss tree die when it ssstill has sssome life in it."

"I am not sure about this, Self-serpent."

"And by the way, my beautiful, sssmart, and kind Eve, how do you think the Master Gardener made it to the master position He is currently in? I will tell you how. He made it by making sssome tough decisions. He knows that the only way you and Adam can ever become your own master gardeners is by believing in the power of your own ssselves. By believing in your own abilities and ssstrengths you both can be the master of your own gardens – masters of your own ssset-apart place. That is really what thisss is all about, Eve. The Master Gardener is afraid that if you sssave thisss tree you won't have to be His ssservants anymore, you will be ssset free!"

"His servants? Set free?"

"Yesss, His ssservants, and yesss, ssset free. Alsssso, Eve, if you and Adam become your own master gardeners then you won't have to answer to Him or be bothered by His ssstrict instructionsss anymore, because you will be able to make your own instructionsss and create your own rulesss."

"Strict instructions? My own rules?"

"Yesss, He hasss given you ssstrict rules. His instructionsss are heavy and burdensssome."

Eve looked bewildered and confused. She began to speak softer than normal, as if she were speaking under her breath. But still, the self-serpent could hear what she was saying.

"Why would the Master Gardener want to keep us from partaking in this tree? It is true that Adam and I partake in all the other trees and they do stay energetic and fresh-looking."

"Yesss, thisss is true."

The self-serpent knew it was beginning to pull the strings of persuasion over Eve. The first obstacle to overcome was getting her to agree on something – on anything – and now, it could say, "check."

"I know you want to sssave this tree. It is not a bad tree, Eve. It just has not been nourished like the others. Don't you think it deserves an opportunity to flourish and be beautiful like you and I? How do you think it feels, knowing that all the other treesss get your'sss and Adam'sss attention, and it doesn't even get a glance?"

Eve still had not committed, but oh, the battle was raging. Something inside of her was saying to run away, and run fast, but would she?

For the first time in her existence, she felt a flood of unfamiliar thoughts and emotions run through her being. It was like a whole world of opportunity was expanding through her mind, and her being was receiving a plethora of endless opportunities.

"Thisss is it, Eve, I've got the perfect idea. You are going to love thisss!"

Eve's countenance began to change as her ears began to perk up.

What if I checked it out? What if I listened more? The Master Gardener did say we were mature enough to learn about 'joined embrace', so why wouldn't I be mature enough to make a wise decision concerning the Tree of the Knowledge of Good and Evil? What if the self-serpent is right? What if the Master Gardener is testing us to see if we have what it takes to become our own master gardeners?

Eve didn't realize that again she was granting the self-serpent access. This time it was access to her thoughts. And because she had granted it access to her thoughts, the door to authority over her mind was now opened too. This weakened her in every way.

Eve's countenance continued to change. It was not for the better. It was for the worse.

Never before have I felt such limitlessness! This must be what the Master Gardener has been hiding from us, and this must be what He Himself experienced when He was becoming His own master gardener. Oh, the endless opportunities that are set before me.

"Yesss! Yes, I will listen, Self-serpent! Tell me more, please, tell me more."

Eve was now speaking the self-serpent's language, and this delighted it all the more, for it knew that very soon it would be receiving praise and esteem for saving the Tree of the Knowledge of Good and Evil.

"Thisss is the plan, Eve. Thisss is how we will sssave the Tree of the Knowledge of Good and Evil."

The self-serpent felt more at ease with Eve and knew all it had to do was share its plan with her and she would make it come to fruition.

"Let me prepare a way for you to partake of the tree without you even having to look upon it. And you do not even have to touch it if you choossse not to."

"But I have already seen that its fruit looks delicious and good to eat."

"Yesss, you have, my dear."

"Of course, it may be good of me to decide not to touch it. I do not want to get my hands dirty, Self-serpent. But please, continue and tell me more."

"My pleasure, my dear! Here's the plan: I will gather some of the tree'sss fruit and make a juice. I will hold the cup that contains the juice, and I will help you partake. Once you partake of the juice from the fruit, the tree will begin to be nourished and will bounce back from itsss withering sssstate. You and I will have sssaved the tree from becoming extinct. I will take the credit, ssso you will not get into trouble with the Master Gardener. He will think I brought it back to life and not be upsssset with you."

"Give you credit so the Master Gardener does not get mad at me? Does He even know that you are here, Self-serpent? Does He know you are inside the Set-Apart Place?"

"Oh, my dear, at this point, it does not even matter. Who caresss if He knowsss I am here or not? And who caresss who getsss the credit for sssaving the tree? As long as it is sssaved, we can all partake in it and enjoy in itsss bounty. Just think, Eve – very sssoon we will be our own master gardenersss! We will be the very onesss who took sssomething that was considered evil and turned it into good."

The self-serpent knew it must seize the moment. It told Eve to stay put while it harvested the fruit and prepared the juice. She obeyed its voice and sat down in a patch of grass near the tree to wait for its return.

As the self-serpent was busy collecting fruit from the tree, it failed to notice that a lamb was approaching. Usually when an animal came near the same path that the self-serpent was on, it would just hiss and they would scatter off. This time, the self-serpent was busy and distracted with its lust for the opportunity to call evil good.

Eve began to hear and feel another being approaching, and she became aware that it was a lamb.

What is it doing here? I don't need something else to deal with right now.

"Hey, lamb, what are you doing over this way?"

Eve wondered if the lamb was breaking out and becoming its own great shepherd, just like she was breaking out and becoming her own master gardener.

The lamb decided to respond to Eve's question with a question.

"What are you doing out here, Eve?"

Why is he questioning me? Does he not know that I can now make my own decisions? That I can now go as I please and discover all there is to explore?

"Eve, you know the Master Gardener instructed you to stay away from this tree."

"Did He? Were you there?" she replied.

The lamb just stood there, waiting for her to come to her senses.

"Who do you think you are, lamb? And why are you getting into my business?"

In her mind, Eve had become mature enough to make her own decisions. But the lamb was all-wise, and he knew what Eve was thinking. He knew that pride and arrogance were stirring in her being. He knew she was captivated by her own self-centered desires.

Saddened by the disrespect that Eve was exhibiting toward her male Adam and her Creator, the lamb decided to establish a second witness to the original instruction given concerning the Tree of the Knowledge of Good and Evil. The lamb took this opportunity to speak its mind, which was in one accord with the Master Gardener.

"Eve, what are you doing hanging out around this tree? You know the Master Gardener warned you to stay away from it. And He designed it with its own unique fragrance as an indicator to those passing by that they should keep going. I know you must have smelled it once you got close."

"Who asked you, lamb?"

The lamb was not deterred and continued to speak.

"The Tree of the Knowledge of Good and Evil is destined to wither away. The Master Gardener knew if it was starved that over time it would begin to wither, then decay. Then, over more time, it would be destroyed. And, over more time, it would become a memory. And, over more time, it would become forgotten. And, over more time, it would remain dead. And, over more time, it would be sealed, never to be resurrected. This is how wise the Master Gardener is. He created His Set-Apart Place to be a garden that would filter out all darkness. Over time, all that would remain would be the good fruits that are worthy of His table, and having found within, those worthy of an invitation to His banquet and worthy to live eternally in His Kingdom."

Eve rolled her eyes. She did not want to hear it.

"This is the desire of the Master Gardener, Eve, and He does accomplish all that He sets out to achieve. The works of darkness and the ability to produce them will be destroyed, and there is no changing this truth."

CHAPTER TWENTY-TWO

THE LOVE OF A LAMB, PART ONE

"Hisss, I'm back. Oh, you are here. Hiss away you little lamb, hiss away. You have no authority here. Eve has decided to help me sssave the Tree of the Knowledge of Good and Evil, and we will be esteemed for it."

The self-serpent was angry with the lamb for being there. But at the same time, it knew to remain calm and in control of the situation. It knew that this lamb had all authority, all wisdom, knowledge, and discernment, and was perfect in every way. It just didn't want that knowledge to be shared with Eve – at least not yet. Not until the self-serpent received its praise for saving the Tree of the Knowledge of Good and Evil would it be willing to uncover who the lamb really was.

With a genuine smile on his face and true joy in his being, the lamb decided to try one more time.

"Eve, let's go. Let's get out of here. Let's go find Adam. Let's see what fun he is having today."

Eve's quietness and stillness quickly saddened the lamb, for he knew what would be ahead of her if she decided to linger there much longer.

As Eve just stood there, full of her own self-pride and arrogance, the lamb stood there too. He loved Eve very much and wanted to rescue her. He wanted her to be empowered by his love and concern. He desired that she understood what was placed before her, and that if she would make the right decision – to leave now – things could be worked on, and she would be granted more time to mature to a level that would cause her to grow in understanding and protect her from ever being in this type of situation again.

The lamb knew that if Eve would choose to run back to what she knew was right, her choice would keep her under the protective covering of the Master Gardener and His Set-Apart Place. But at the same time, the lamb also knew that Eve could not be forced to do anything that was against her own will. The Master Gardener had designed it that way because He wanted His creation to want to do right, without having to be forced. And, although the lamb knew Eve was under the influence of the voice of the self-serpent, and that she was about to make the worst decision of her life, he was not willing to leave her.

As the lamb and Eve continued to converse back and forth, she became argumentative with him. All the while, the lamb continued to express true love and humility. As Eve's emotional state began to fly out of control, the lamb continued to give the example of meekness. As she began to yell, he began to grow quiet. As she became more stubborn, he became filled with grief. As she made her decision, he felt the pain of being forsaken.

The lamb stood there with tears welling in his eyes. They soon began to overflow and make droplets that reached the ground, entering the rich, nutrient-dense soil. The Set-Apart Place had never been touched by this type of liquid before. Its soil was now mixed with life that sprouted forth and grief that was birthed from sadness.

The lamb's heartache was great, but he still did not want to leave Eve. He loved her. With a puddle of tears moistening the ground around him, he remained and watched her partake of the Tree of the Knowledge of Good and Evil.

Chapter Twenty-Three

TAINTED FRUIT JUICE

Eve was caught off guard by the lamb's compassion. She briefly second-guessed her decision, but then quickly passed it off.

The lamb has no business being here, trying to persuade me of anything. There is nothing wrong with doing the right thing. There is nothing wrong with helping the self-serpent save this tree. And furthermore, when I do, I will be rewarded. I am not going to let the self-serpent take all the credit for saving the most 'in dire need of saving' tree in all the Earth. The Tree of the Knowledge of Good and Evil will be saved, and I will soon have the power to be in full authority over my own garden. I will soon be my own master gardener!

Thoughts of freedom rushed through Eve's being and they began to nurture her desires for independence from the Master Gardener. Adding entitlement to the mixture that was brewing inside her, she now coveted a new way of living that would allow her to be her own governor.

Now I can pride myself in knowing that I am an independent thinker and decision-maker. I love the Master Gardener and Adam, but I need my own identity apart from them. They do not make up who I really am, nor can they unlock my true potential. That is up to me. I am the one who will now make my own decisions, even if they are not here to counsel me. I am complete and intelligent without them. Yes, Adam was created ahead of me, but that does not lessen the awesomeness of my independence and uniqueness. Yes, the Master Gardener was once who I took instructions from, but now, I make my own rules. This is my life. I am my own greatness. And I am now going to take control of this situation, gain wisdom and authority while doing it, and then convince Adam that this is the right thing to do.

"Here it is, my good friend, Eve. Here is the juice I promised. Thank you for your empathy toward thisss tree. And what great wisdom you have! You have been wise enough to sssee that thisss tree deserves sssaving."

"I am ready, Self-serpent. I am ready to partake of the fruit from the Tree of the Knowledge of Good and Evil. I am already experiencing the effects of the wisdom and knowledge that will be poured into me, for I am making the decision to help save this tree."

I will be my own master gardener very soon, and Adam will be so proud of me too. If he is not, then I will know that he is just jealous of me because I got the opportunity to save this tree before he did.

"Yesss, I agree with what the wise and knowledgeable Eve is sssaying! Do what thou will and let it be so!"

The lamb kept quiet while great sadness gripped his being. Watching Eve made him sick, and yet he was still determined not to leave her. He knew she had made the decision to drink the tree's juice long before this moment. He knew he had tried to stop her, and now he knew he must witness what she was about to do.

Having already welcomed in the voice of the self-serpent, Eve now had no qualms about welcoming its touch too. Coiling its way up her being, the self-serpent slithered up Eve's legs, encircled her torso and positioned itself to lead her further astray.

"Hisss, my beautiful friend. Thisss is the juice you have been waiting for. Thisss is the juice that will make you your own master gardener. Open wide that I may asssist you in fulfilling your desires to sssave this tree."

The self-serpent held its grip firm around Eve's being while gently cupping her head in one hand and pouring the tainted juice into her mouth with its other. And, as she began to drink the juice, Eve felt a rush of entitlement and pride welling up within her being.

The lamb watched as Eve's light began to dim and grow bright and then dim and grow bright again. This fluctuation in Eve's light continued while she drank the juice. And as Eve drank, out of the corner of her eye she spotted the lamb watching her and the self-serpent.

He's still here!

Eve assumed the lamb would have gone about his business. She thought by now he should be tarrying on down the path, back to the Tree of Life where he'd been known to hang out, but he wasn't. He was still standing there, observing, being present but quiet.

As tears began to well up in her eyes, she questioned, *Why is he still here?* But she continued to drink the juice anyway. And for a few seconds, which felt like moments, she could feel waves of guilt, shame, entitlement, and pride stirring within her being.

It's the lamb! It's the lamb's fault I'm experiencing these feelings of guilt and shame. It is because he is watching me.

All these thoughts plagued Eve's mind until she could no longer keep quiet. She paused drinking, lifted her head up halfway from the position it was being held in, and yelled, "Go away, lamb!"

"Oh, Eve, dear, pay the little lambie no attention. He's just jealous. Here, dear – go ahead and finish your drink."

Eve continued to listen to the self-serpent's voice, and as she was finishing her drink a spirit of anger began to grow within her being. Having consumed the juice, she lifted her head and boisterously blurted, "Wow, lamb, this is great stuff! Wanna try some?"

"Hisss. Oh, yesss, dear, I do like your idea. I do think the little lambie should try sssome."

Eve wiped the tears from her eyes. She was now an emotional mess.

"It was ssso sssweet and enjoyable to my tassste budsss."

Eve could not move past the immediate desire and addiction she had acquired for the taste of the juice from the fruit of the Tree of the Knowledge of Good and Evil. The very idea that the Master Gardener did not want this tree to be saved was now ludicrous in her eyes. She quickly became enraged at the Master Gardener and began to think that He was not as smart or as honest as she had originally thought.

The self-serpent slithered down Eve's body, releasing her from their embrace.

"Hisss, you like, do you, hisss?"

"Hell yesss, I like! And I want more. Thank you for introducing me to this powerfully potent tree! There is nothing wrong with Adam and me consuming fruit from this tree! The Master Gardener has been lying to us. We should be consuming the fruit of this tree every single day."

"Of course you should, dear," the self-serpent replied.

"No longer will this tree be neglected while all the others are not!" Eve added.

"Yesss, I agree with my dearly beloved and beautiful Eve. And you will make a great master gardener! You already have me in agreement with your desiresss. There will be more in agreement with your desiresss too, just watch."

The moments of Eve's betrayal to the Master Gardener and Adam had now passed, and yet she still didn't want to leave the presence of the self-serpent nor the Tree of the Knowledge of Good and Evil.

"Go away, lamb! You are not wanted around here!"

Her tears were now dried up and although Eve's inner light was ever so slightly and gradually dimming, she could not see it for herself.

"And I second that persssonal witnesss of my good friend Eve'sss desire. Go away!"

Although the lamb could not have cared less for the self-serpent's desires or commands, he turned around and began to leave because of Eve's. Because of her desires, the lamb turned and left.

CHAPTER TWENTY-FOUR
WHERE'S EVE?

Adam found himself searching for Eve all over the Set-Apart Place.

"Eve, Eve! Where are you?" he yelled.

He had already stopped to ask several of the animals if they had seen his Eve. They all said they had not. After deciding to turn onto a trail that he hardly ever took, Adam heard a noise that caught his attention.

Maybe it is Eve, he thought, but soon realized it was not.

"The lamb! Behold the lamb! How are you doing today, lamb?" he asked.

With red eyes, the lamb looked up at Adam.

"Friend, I have had better days."

"It is odd seeing you this far from the Tree of Life, lamb. Are you okay?"

"Like I said, friend, I have had better days, but it will all get worked out over time," he said. Then the lamb continued on, making his way back to the Tree of Life.

Adam was curious about what the lamb had meant when he said, *it will all get worked out over time,* but because the lamb kept moving, Adam did too. And before long, he ran into his love.

"Eve! There you are! Where have you been? And what have you been up to? I had no idea you would wander off on this path. I have been searching for you everywhere. You are getting good at hiding."

Adam joyfully reached out to embrace his Eve, but she did not reciprocate fully. Having a bit of a snobbish spirit, she was colder than normal, and Adam could feel a difference in her vibe.

"What is wrong, my Eve? I have never felt this coolness from you before. And your light, it is dimming! Are you okay?"

"Yes, Adam, I am wonderful. I have never been better, and with time, my better will become my best. And as far as my light goes, I no longer need that old thing anyway. I am going to create my own brightness and become my own light."

"Hmm, okay." Adam was puzzled. "Well, I do not know what you are talking about when you say 'with time your better will become your best,' but maybe I should look into this 'time' thing, because this word keeps being brought to my attention. And yes, Eve, you very much do need your light, for several reasons."

"Adam, neither of us knows what the other one is talking about. This is a waste of my time!"

"Ugh! There it is again ... '*time*.' What is going on?"

Eve began to walk off.

"Wait, Eve! Please don't go. We need to meet the Master Gardener in the avocado orchards."

Eve rolled her eyes at Adam.

"What now?" she said.

"What do you mean, 'what now?'" he replied.

The level of frustration Adam was experiencing was unfamiliar to him. He had never known it before and did not understand the wave of confusion mixed with frustration that coursed through his being.

"And where is all this sarcasm coming from? All I know about sarcasm is that it is a fruit that resides on the Tree of the Knowledge of Good and Evil and it should be left alone, Eve, left alone to decay. So why are you exhibiting it?"

"Okay, Adam, you want to bring up decaying? Let me tell you something."

Eve pointed back in the direction of the Tree of the Knowledge of Good and Evil.

"This tree should not be decaying. We should be trying to save it. It probably produces negative fruit because it has been neglected for way too long!"

"Eve! What are you talking about? Where is my sweet helpmate? You did not partake of the Tree of the Knowledge of Good and Evil, did you?"

"So what if I did, Adam? So what if I did!"

"I knew it!"

Adam's countenance immediately fell, and he responded in an emotion he had never embraced or had words for.

"Eve, please tell me what happened. We need to fix this."

"There is nothing to be fixed. I am better than ever! Didn't you hear me the first time? Furthermore, to fill you in, I decided to do the right thing and show compassion to this decaying tree. And now that I have, I have been blessed with secret wisdom and knowledge to course my own path – to be my own master gardener!"

"But Eve, why? Why did you do this?"

"I am not lying to you, Adam – I am now better than ever, and you can be too."

"I cannot believe you did this," he responded. Adam then cupped his hands over his face, tilted his head toward the ground, and began to cry.

Eve stood there with dismay on her face. She could not understand why Adam was responding to her delight in such a grievous manner.

Why is he crying! Hmph, he is so weak, she thought.

"I enjoyed our life, Eve, I really did. I enjoyed the way it was – growing and learning from the Master Gardener at a pace that nurtured each of our stages, as we ripen to maturity. I was really looking forward to what the Master Gardener was about to teach us. We were going to learn how to be fruitful and multiply the seed of our union."

Tears continued to run down Adam's face.

"I am glad that you are happy about this change in you, but I will miss our life together, for we will no longer be equally yoked."

While Adam's head hung low from his broken heart, Eve continued to exhibit a nature that had been foreign to them both. There was no questioning the difference in her demeanor, although Adam's sadness did cause her to briefly think back on the days of innocence she had once shared with him.

We have had fun together in this garden, dancing with the butterflies and singing harmonious melodies with the beautiful birds, chasing the lightning bugs ...

Then suddenly, Eve snapped out of her reminiscing.

I am an independent female now, a woman of authority. Yeah, that is what I will tell him! He needs to know this about me!

"Adam, you need to know this. I am new and I am different. I am a new, different, and better version of myself. I am an independent female now, Adam, and I will no longer wait around for you to make decisions for me."

Adam and Eve were now standing face-to-face in arm's reach. Their conversation was getting heated, and something began to boil within Adam's being. He became very bothered, to the point that he was ready to push Eve away – which is exactly what he did.

Throwing his arms out in the air and pushing her away, Adam turned his back on his female and began to walk away. Looking back over his shoulder he blurted, "You want your independence, Eve, you take it! It's yours! Just leave me be!"

Eve became startled and uncertain.

"Adam, wait! You are leaving me?"

"Eve, I have got to go!"

But this time Adam wasn't yelling over his shoulder, nor was he looking back. He was now moving straight forward, away from the situation and away from the one who had broken his heart.

"Wait, Adam!" Eve yelled as she dashed towards him and grabbed the back of his shoulder.

"Eve, I have nothing to wait for. Leave me be!"

"Adam, wait. I cannot believe you are being like this!"

At this point, Adam was incredibly enraged. He knew Eve had become double-minded, saying one thing one minute, and another thing the next. And while Adam was enraged, Eve was dumbfounded.

Wow, I did not know this would cause my male to be so upset with me. He sure is being double-minded. He says I am his love, and then he just treats me like this! Hmph.

Eve wanted her independence, but she was also quickly realizing she could not live without the adoration of her male. It was important to her. Without it, jealousy would plague Eve, and she knew it.

"Adam, I cannot believe you are just going to walk away. You have never left me like this!"

Adam stopped in his tracks and turned towards her. He could no longer resist the temptation to argue.

"Eve, I have to go. I need to meet with the Master Gardener in the avocado orchards!"

"Why are you going to meet with the Master Gardener anyway? You never did tell me that."

"I don't have to tell you anything anymore. I owe you nothing! And it is sad how dumb you have become now that you have eaten from that rotten tree. How easily you forget that I meet with Him every day. What is wrong with you?"

I have never seen him like this, Eve thought. *What is wrong with him? He should be glad for me, for us! For now we have the opportunity to become our best. Hmph, no respect. I guess his true colors were bound to come through at some point. He doesn't care for me. All he cares about is the Master Gardener. I am no priority to him, hmph.*

"Well, Adam, that should change. And, by the way, it's not even time for the second daily communion – the Greater Light is not setting. Looks like the Master Gardener is requiring more and more of your time. Hmph. Your twice daily is now turning into thrice daily. You have not even begun to know the control He has over you, Adam."

Suddenly, as if giving up the fight but not the argument, Adam's voice began to grow soft, and Eve had to move closer just to hear what he was saying.

"Eve, I do not know what the meeting is about, but I just know I need to be there. I know it's not our regularly scheduled meeting time, but my heart is broken, and I am all confused. I do not even know what is happening to me, but I do know the One Who can help me."

"The Master Gardener cannot help you, Adam. Only you can help yourself!"

"Eve, I am done. I do not want to listen to you any longer. Get out of my face!"

Eve was beginning to panic.

I must stop him from leaving me. I need to be the number one in his life, not The Master Gardener.

Eve reached out to touch Adam on the arm in an attempt to persuade him to stay.

"Adam, please stop, please wait. The Master Gardener is not as trustworthy as you may think. Remember, He has known we were mature enough to learn about joined embrace, and yet He still has not brought it up to us. Do you not think that is wrong? And do you not think He should have taught us about it before now?"

"Eve, I am the one who just recently brought up the subject about being fruitful and multiplying. After that is when the Master Gardener said we could talk about it very soon. That is probably what He had in mind to talk to us about this afternoon."

Adam was exhausted from what he was experiencing and did not have the strength to respond any longer, nor did he have the desire to argue. Again, he turned to walk away, and again Eve reached out to try and stop him, for a spirit of jealousy had begun to rise within her being.

Oh my, what is going on? He is really walking away from me. I better do something and do it quick, she thought.

"Please stay here, Adam. Please hear me out. I have a plan. And if you will just trust me, you will begin to understand. I am sorry, my love. I am sorry I made you cry. Please do not go. Please stay."

Adam's heartstrings were torn. His head was spinning, and the longer he listened to Eve's voice the more he found himself being drawn toward her request.

"My love, can you please just hold off from going to that meeting? Please, Adam, meet with me instead. I need you. If you will just give me a little bit of your time, you will soon understand."

While Adam was devastated and weak, Eve took this moment to put her hands around his lower waist and draw him closer to her. Then she continued to speak softly and tenderly to him.

"Please meet with me instead, my love. Meet me and the self-serpent under the Tree of the Knowledge of Good and Evil. We will have it make us some more of that sweet juice from the tree's fruit. You can consume like I did, and we will no longer be unequally yoked."

"So that is what you did, and that is how it happened?"

"Yes, my love, that is what I did, and that is how it happened. The self-serpent prepared some juice from the fruit of the Tree of the Knowledge of Good and Evil, and I drank it."

While Eve continued to speak softly to him, Adam was becoming a mental mess. He could no longer think straight. He became foggy-headed and continued to weaken physically. And although he was trying to stay strong, he was also beginning to slip. He was beginning to succumb to a nature that, up until this point, had been foreign to him.

Maybe I should, maybe I shouldn't, he thought.

"What are you doing to me, Eve? My head is spinning and I feel faint. I told the Master Gardener I would meet with Him. I gave Him my word."

"But I am your helpmate, Adam, and we are one. Is it fair that I always must do what you want? Does it not work both waysss? I do not ask much of you, Adam. Just this once, please, you will sssee that it is not a bad tree and that it does not deserve the neglect it has been receiving."

Eve batted her eyes and twirled a lock of her hair with her finger, all the while looking up at her male and being thrilled to have found a new way to manipulate him into making her desires come true.

"Besides, don't forget the conversation in our tree house recently, where you said it would be great for me to make some decisions about how we ssspend our days."

CHAPTER TWENTY-FIVE

THE FALL OF ADAM

"Eve!"

Adam didn't understand why or how he was so easily losing control.

"I told the Master Gardener we would be there. Our absence would greatly concern Him. If you are not going, then at least, I need to show up."

Adam's mind was flooded with unfamiliar thoughts. He had never contemplated what it would be like to leave the Master Gardener hanging. As he began to be led by the pull of Eve's hand, he wondered, *Will I ever be the same after this?*

While Eve was leading Adam to the Tree of the Knowledge of Good and Evil, mixed emotions and new feelings began to stir within his being. Something inside of him said that this was wrong – very wrong – but still, he could not stop himself from following Eve's lead.

The sober-mindedness and strength that Adam once knew and walked in was now fading into a clouded memory. His light was beginning to dim, but he was not aware of it.

As Eve began to pick up her pace, she grew in a spirit of control.

Finally, I am in the lead now, and I will enjoy every minute of it!

"Slow down, my love. Slow down," Adam puffed.

"Okay, Adam, my male, I will slow down. We are almost there anyway."

"Good," he responded.

Eve took pride in knowing she was now a quick learner, and she was quickly learning how to use her speech and body movements to manipulate her male.

"Okay, here we are."

Adam gave Eve an eye roll.

"I knew by the smell."

"Yeah, it smells great, doesn't it? The smell of power!"

"Hisss, hello, hisss hisss."

"Hello, Self-serpent," Eve said.

"Hello, my friend Eve. Hello, Adam," it replied.

The self-serpent knew it was just a matter of time before Adam would be its friend too.

Adam rolled his eyes again.

"Eve! You are friends now? Are they even supposed to be in the Set-Apart Place?"

"Adam, I don't know what you are talking about. Look at this beautiful, kind, and helpful being, and don't be so judgmental. You really should free yourself from that."

"Eve! A self-serpent, um ... This cannot be good, Eve."

"Oh, Adam, it is not that big of a deal. You have friends, so why shouldn't I? Besides, this one is beautiful, just like me and you, my love." At Adam's look she quickly added, "I know what you are thinking, Adam, and no, it is not evil. This is the one who helped set me free. And yes, I have heard you and the Master Gardener talk about the various beings that live beyond the border of the Fence-of-Fire, but this one is different."

"Different?"

"Yes, different, and in a good way. Are you not the least bit interested in getting to know it?"

"Eve, you are avoiding my question."

"I answered your question. Yes, we are friends."

"The other question."

"What question?"

"Ugh!"

"Lighten up, Adam."

"In this place, Eve! Is it supposed to be in this set-apart place?"

Although Adam knew the answer in his heart, he still demanded one from Eve.

"Can't you see, Adam? I am already smarter than you, for I partook in this tree, and it has made me wise. You can't even keep up with my mental intelligence. And yes, Self-serpent is supposed to be here."

"In the Set-Apart Place?"

"Yes, my love, in the Set-Apart Place!"

"Really? I did not know it was able to pass over the Fence-of-Fire."

"Well, now you do!"

"You gave it permission?"

"Yes, I did! And I am glad that I did. This beautiful and smart being has helped set me free!"

"Set you free, seriously? I did not know that was a need of yours."

Adam began to laugh out loud.

"Well, yes it was, and I was also in need of a true friend. You can keep the mocking to yourself."

"Eve, you have true friends, you always have. All the animals love you! When you do not tag along with me, they always ask me how you are doing. I have also seen you playing with them. The koala bear loves to play with you in the meadows. The raccoons help you gather veggies in the garden, and you love rolling down the grassy knolls with the playful deer. Do not tell me you don't have friends."

"Those were my old friends, Adam. I am mature now and do not have time for that kind of childish behavior. I was thinking that instead of playing with the animals I could start having them work for us, so we can really get some things accomplished around here."

Adam let out a sigh of frustration as he asked her the next question. "Eve, what are you talking about?"

"Well, Adam, since I have been blessed by drinking the juice from the fruit of the Tree of the Knowledge of Good and Evil, my mind has been opened to endless possibilities, and they are in our favor, Adam. Do you hear me? *They are in our favor*. One of the things I am going to do is become my own master gardener. And since I am now capable of giving orders, my mind is coming up with all these different ideas about how the animals can help me reach my goals."

"Goals?"

"Do not interrupt me, Adam, I am speaking. Yes, my goals. I know that is a new concept for you, but it is all about reaching and rising to be the best I can be now. I am no longer going to apologize for it. And you might as well know I am developing these thoughts in my mind. They are awesome thoughts, thoughts about the animals taking orders from us."

"Eve, I am interrupting you now! The animal beings are to be loved, nurtured, and respected."

"Think about it, Adam. The ostrich is fast. It could deliver messages for us in little to no time."

"There is that word again, *time*. Ugh! Why are you talking such nonsense? Where is my Eve?"

"You are interrupting me again. Can I get a little respect? And can you please focus? Now, back to what I was saying: the elephants can dig in the soil with their tusks and pull heavy loads. The grizzly bears can clean out the caves in case we would like to enjoy one for a romantic getaway."

"Romantic getaway? What is that?"

Eve then brought her hands up towards Adam's face and snapped her fingers.

"Keep listening, Adam. I will teach you what 'romantic getaway' means later. The horses and donkeys could carry loads for us, making our chores easier. The birds can be our couriers. The dogs could chase the cats away, and the cats could chase the mice away, when we do not want to be bothered with them."

"Bothered?"

The self-serpent was getting impatient listening to Adam and Eve go on and on. It had a mission to fulfill, and time was wasting, so it decided to speak up.

"Getting parched, are we? I have a new recipe to share. The juice I made for you, dear, was wonderfully sssweet, and I know you enjoyed it. But now I have come up with a better blend."

"Better blend? I enjoyed the first blend. What are you talking about, Self-serpent?"

The self-serpent lit up with uncanny excitement.

"Eve, I am glad you asked! Let me fill you and my new friend Adam in, on my new recipe. When I was gathering fruit from the Tree of the Knowledge of Good and Evil to make juice for you, Eve, I only gathered a few of the variousss fruitsss, and look how beneficial it wasss for you. Look how just those few fruitsss have given you great knowledge and wisssdom.

"Sssince we have been talking about being our bessst and becoming our own master gardenersss, I too have been blesssed with great knowledge and wisssdom that flowsss from a heart that desssires my friendsss Adam and Eve to alssso become the bessst that they can be. I have come up with the mossst wonderful idea. If those few fruitsss have opened the doorsss for thisss much wisssdom to flow to you, Eve, think about the magnitude of tasssting all the tree'sss fruitsss and its leavesss. Think about the endlesss posssibilitiesss that would flood your mindsss and your beingsss. You truly would have the capacity to reach your highessst potential."

"Wow! I was not thinking of that, Self-serpent, but I am glad you brought it to our attention. Truly, Self-serpent, you are more than beautiful, you are all-wise! I am so thankful you are willing to help us reach our highessst potential now and not later. I mean, I know the Master Gardener cares for us, but he says that we benefit ourselves and others by growing patiently, and that just does not make sense to me anymore, when we can become mature beingsss right here and now."

"I don't know about this, Eve. We have always trusted the Master Gar—"

"Adam, that's just it!" Eve interjected. "We have put our trust in someone other than our own ssselves, and by doing so it has locked us into a long road. The way of the Master Gardener is slow and steady. I am ready for fast and fabulous. I am ready to achieve my goals now. I am ready to be ripe and mature now, not later."

Eve knew she was getting too excited for Adam's comfort, and she also knew she needed to calm herself down, in order for her to take control of the situation.

I know. I will take advantage of my new skill of manipulation. Adam will not be able to resist.

"Come here, handsome. There is something I want to whisssper in your ear."

At this point, Adam could no longer resist, for he had become entangled in a battle that was too strong for him.

"Adam, my love," Eve breathed in his ear. "I know you are the leader of our union. I remember the day I awoke to be forever by your side. You are the most important being in my existence. When you told me you would miss me because we were becoming unequally yoked, well, it was almost too much for me to bear. You are me, Adam. I came from you. And I am you, my love. I am your extension. I am all that extends from your being. All that could not fit into your being does my being house. Let usss stay one, my love, please."

Adam's being lit up with excitement.

Finally, she is giving me some respect, he thought.

Adam appreciated that Eve was acknowledging him as being the leader of their union, as the thought of their separation had begun to pang him deeply.

Don't forget to keep batting your eyes, Eve, and twirling a lock of your hair. Remember, he loves your long, beautiful, and curling hair, she thought.

Adam could no longer hold back his newfound passions. It was as if he was lovesick and nothing else mattered.

"My love! My Eve! What are you doing to me?" he asked for the second time.

This manipulation thing is really working. Hmph, who would have thought? I wonder which one he likes best: batting my eyes or twirling the locks of my hair? I wonder which one is more powerful?

"What is happening? You are causing a change in me. I am so thankful for your adoration. I agree, you are me, and I am you. I never should have even thought about us being unequally yoked. Please forgive me. This union we have is so powerful, and you are right: we can be our own master gardeners. Tell me what I must do, my love. Tell me what I must do, pleassse."

Never before had Adam experienced such a pull towards Eve. Not only had his mind weakened but also his entire being.

Why is this happening? What is going on? he thought.

Adam was trying to stay strong and alert, but he was weakening very quickly.

"Adam, my love, my strong and fearless leader, drink the juice of the fruit of the Tree of the Knowledge of Good and Evil and together let usss reach our highest potential. And let usss not forget the compassion we will be sharing with the less-fortunate tree. Remember that this tree needs usss. It needs our help to survive! We will be doing a great thing by drinking its juice and helping it bounce back to life."

"And tea from the leavesss, don't forget thossse," the self-serpent interjected.

"Yes, absolutely, Self-serpent. And Adam, just think about it – we will cause this tree to live and not die. This tree can be saved from the grip of destruction. It can thrive. Just as we have blessed the other trees in this set-apart place, we can bless the Tree of the Knowledge of Good and Evil. Now let's be heroes and save the less fortunate, let us cause this tree to flourish!"

Eve was nestled in the grips of Adam's embrace, while it was Adam that felt consumed by the power of her presence.

"Hisss," they heard coming from outside their embrace.

"What is it, Ssself-serpent?" they responded in unison.

"Thisss is it. While you two lovebirdsss were getting acquainted, I was gathering the fruit and leavesss of the neglected tree. I have made tea from the leavesss and have mixed it with the juice of all the variousss fruitsss that were on the branches of the limbsss, as we discusssed. I sssampled sssome myself, and it is very tasty, tasty indeed."

"I know we are going to be so blessed by this tree. I am going to drink the juice mixed with the tea, with my male Adam, for I only experienced a few varieties of the tree's fruit before. And I want it all too, just like my male Adam."

"No problem with that on thisss end," the self-serpent said.

"Wow. Think about it, Adam – we get to experience all the various fruits from the tree, mixed with the tea from its many leaves. It is sure to make us the wisest of all, wiser than the animals and maybe wiser than the Master Gardener Himself!"

This is when the self-serpent seized its moment and began to slither up Eve's leg. And, within a few brief moments it had crossed over to Adam's. Then it continued to coil around the couple, spiraling up and down their embrace.

"This is it, my lovesss. Thisss is the juice mixed with the tea you have been waiting for. Thisss drink will turn both of you into your own master gardenersss. Now tilt your headsss back and open wide that I may asssist you in fulfilling your desssires."

"We are ready, Self-serpent," Eve said. "We are ready to partake of the juice mixed with the tea. We are already experiencing the effects of the wisdom and knowledge that will be poured into us, for we are making the decision to help save this tree. We will be our own master gardeners very soon, and all the animals will praise us for being wise enough to figure out how to save this tree. And if they do not praise us, it is only because they are jealous that we thought to save the tree before they did."

Adam held Eve's tilted head in his hands as she opened her mouth.

"'Ladies firssst' worked lassst time, ssso we will try that again," the self-serpent said, as it began pouring the drink into Eve's mouth.

While Eve's head and upper being leaned back, and she was taking in all her portion, out of the corner of her eye, she saw the lamb.

That stupid lamb again! He came back! she thought.

At this point, Adam was not aware of the lamb standing off to the side. And although he saw a tear well up in Eve's eye, he had no idea what that meant.

Eve finished her portion of the drink and then Adam gently helped guide her neck and head back into a straight position. Adam noticed that she was now wearing an uncanny grin. This disturbed him greatly, but he was powerless, so much to the point that he didn't even question her over it.

Unknowing of what would lie ahead of them, Adam and Eve were captured in the moment of their demise. They had no cares or concerns outside of their embrace with the self-serpent.

"It is your turn, my fearlesss friend Adam. Now tilt your head back, open your mouth wide, and I will help you fulfill all your desiresss," the self-serpent said as it slithered further up the couple's embrace, preparing to minister Adam his portion.

Being under a spell for the first time in his life, Adam was now following the instructions of other voices. It first began when he had followed Eve to the Tree of the Knowledge of Good and Evil. Now, this other voice was coming from the self-serpent, but Adam did not care. He had lost all capabilities to hear outside of the trio's embrace.

Obeying the voice of the self-serpent, Adam leaned his head back and opened his mouth wide. And it was in this moment that the spirits of entitlement, pride, and arrogance began to flood into his being, causing him to become irritated, irritated at the Master Gardener.

"Tassste and see that it is good, my friend, hisss," the self-serpent said.

"Yes, my love, drink it all in and enjoy," Eve added.

Why hasn't the Master Gardener taught me the truth about this tree? Why has He been trying to hide this from Eve and me? Truly, Eve must be right about the Master Gardener. He really does not want us learning much, does He? He really wants to keep us sheltered and cut off from all these new and amazing possibilities that lie before us.

While Adam's head was tilted back, he began to be overwhelmed with an odd feeling. He felt as if he was being watched, and it really bothered him. Being watched would never have bothered Adam before, nor would he have taken notice of it. But today it was a new encroaching and uncomfortable feeling.

Adam drank almost all his portion, and then he paused to think back on the conversation he had held with the lamb earlier, when the lamb had said, 'it will all get worked out in time.' He was also thinking about what Eve had said, 'in time, she would become her best.'

"Jussst a little more, my friend," the self-serpent said.

"It is okay, my love, you can finish," Eve said.

So, this must be the awesome, wonderful 'time' everyone is talking about! I like this 'time' we are having. I could stay here in this 'time' all the time, Adam thought, and then he finished his portion of drink.

The feeling of being watched had quickly faded into the background for Adam. Within a few short minutes he had become a male with no concerns. Having finished his drink he then began to lift his neck and head up straight, while realizing that he was now wearing the same uncanny grin on his face that Eve wore when she had finished her portion.

"Wow, that drink really isss powerful," Adam said.

"Yesss, my love!" Eve responded.

"It really does have the power to make usss think and be as one united," the self-serpent said.

"Agreed," Adam said.

"Yesss, my love, and now we can truly be one." Eve said. "We can now be equally yoked forever, no matter what! Because we have joined our desires to save the Tree of the Knowledge of Good and Evil, we can now conquer and fulfill all our desires! It is going to be wonderful."

CHAPTER TWENTY-SIX

THE VIOLATIONS

Both Adam and Eve were captivated by their new thoughts and desires, which had driven away all evidence of innocence and purity. This made the self-serpent very pleased, for it knew that they would now be producing the fruits of what was previously meant to be destroyed.

And, although all three accomplished what they had agreed to do, not one of them wanted to be released from the other's embrace. Eve enjoyed being in Adam's arms, as did he with her. And neither was bothered by the self-serpent's presence.

During their next few moments together, Adam gently whispered in Eve's ear, then he abruptly stopped.

"Our lights! Our lights dim and then shine bright again," he said, while feeling alarmed.

"It is okay, my love. It is normal. We are transssscending to our higher ssselves," Eve soothed.

"Huh?" Adam asked.

"It is normal. Relax. Your light did the same thing while you were drinking from the Tree of the Knowledge of Good and Evil."

"It did?"

"Yes, my love, it did."

"Well, I have not told you until now, but yours did too, my love."

"See, I told you it is normal. It is to be expected, so take it easy and give me a kiss."

"You give *me* a kiss!"

Adam and Eve were enjoying their intimate time together with the self-serpent.

"Yesss, thisss is fun, my lovesss," the self-serpent said.

CHAPTER TWENTY-SEVEN

THE LOVE OF A LAMB, PART TWO

T he moments of Adam and Eve's violations had passed. Adam was trying to relax from all the excitement, but his mind was racing, working against any shalom his being had ever known. This too was a new experience for Adam, and it frustrated him. His mind had always been in sync with his being, but in this moment, his mind was exploding with new thoughts and concepts, new understandings and beliefs, new opportunities and new pathways. The list went on and on. He wanted his mind to slow down for a minute so he could gather his thoughts, but it would not. He had lost control over what he once held in perfect balance.

Eve spoke up to break the silence.

"It is okay, my love, I know what you are going through. Just try and relax. I know your thoughts are spinning out of control, but that is just a part of becoming who we are meant to be. Now that we have set ourselves free to be our own master gardeners, of course our minds are going to be flooded with all sorts of thoughts, concepts, and information."

"I am just not sure that they are the right thoughts, concepts, and information," Adam said.

"Of course they are the right thoughts, Adam! We are empowered now. Because we have made the decision to free our minds and wills, we have been flooded with information that was not previously available to us. I know it is a little overwhelming at first, but we will be better for it, in time."

"Ugh!"

"What?"

"That word again!"

"What word?"

"Time!"

Eve was becoming frustrated with Adam.

"Oh, yeah, I forgot that you are confused over that word," she said.

"What?" Adam responded.

"Puzzled."

"What are you talking about, Eve?"

"Never mind ..."

Adam believed Eve was trying to be encouraging, but it was not helping him. The further the release from the embrace they had all once shared, the further Adam was led into feelings for which he had no words. And although the intimate embrace was over, the memory of it still consumed him, but not in a good way. Waves of questions began to swell in his being.

I felt so good a minute ago. Now, all I feel is—

Adam could not finish his thought.

The lamb! Behold the lamb!

It had been there the whole time, off to the side, watching.

Adam immediately felt guilt and shame, while disgust began to flood every fiber of his being. As high as he was during the trio's embrace, this time he felt as low as he could possibly ever go. Minutes ago, he was lost in his desires. Now, all he wanted to do was cover himself and hide.

When Eve saw the shame on Adam's countenance, she became irritated at the lamb. She knew the lamb had interrupted Adam's pleasant time, and she was going to let him have it.

"Go away, stupid lamb! Why are you hanging out here? You are not wanted here! Go away!"

"Eve, that is a little rough, don't you think?"

"Oh, Adam, from now on all beings will take orders from us. We are the wisest of all beings now, and we are the true ones, for we have saved the Tree of the Knowledge of Good and Evil. No other being has ever come this far. Enjoy the moment and embrace our abilities to be our own master gardeners. Let us make our own rules and ignore that stupid lamb."

"I cannot ignore this lamb, Eve. He has always been my friend. We have had a special bond from the beginning."

"Are you serious? Come on, Adam, that is ridiculous."

"It is true, Eve!" Adam retorted. "This lamb is the very first animal that the Master Gardener gave me to name, and I named him. I gave him his name. And I have always been so blessed by being in his presence ... until now. Now, everything has changed, and it is different. I feel so dirty, Eve, and it's like I never even knew what that word meant until now. How is my mind receiving all these new words and understandings?"

Adam cupped his hands over his face and began to sob. To Eve, Adam was just rambling and showing signs of weakness.

I have got to take control of this situation, she thought.

"Stupid lamb! What does his name mean anyway, and why are you so upset over it?"

"Eve, his name means 'this breath purifies what is to be revealed'."

"What? Why did you name him that? Are you crazy?!"

Adam did not even have to ask what "crazy" was. He rolled his eyes, hissed, and just knew.

"Eve! I honestly cannot tell you why that name came to me. But now, every time I see him, I see *the breath that purifies what is going to be revealed.*"

Eve was upset with Adam for being so concerned about the lamb. She didn't understand their friendship, but what she did believe was that it was time for Adam to get a new set of friends.

"You are right, Adam. I was a little rough on the lamb," she acquiesced. "But it was only because I felt like he should not have been partaking in our private moments."

Adam let out a grievous sigh, for he knew that he had never before needed privacy for any of his actions. He and Eve had always been shown consideration for their personal space, coming from all the animals inside the Set-Apart Place. He had never felt the need, ever, before then, to require privacy for private moments. He now knew that he was on a downhill slide.

The lamb walked closer to Adam, Eve, and the self-serpent, and stood there, staring at them.

Adam's head hung down, and tears started to fall. Without even looking up, he began to softly speak. "Lamb, what are you doing here?"

With no hesitation the lamb responded.

"The Master Gardener said you had plans to meet Him in the avocado orchards. When you didn't show, He knew you were lost, so He sent me to find you. He desires that you return to Him."

Eve quickly grabbed Adam by the arm and made him look her in the eyes while she spoke authoritatively to him.

"Adam, you will not return to the Master Gardener. You are your own master gardener now, and you make your own decisions. Do not heed the voice of the one you once followed when you were weak, for you now follow the voice within your own ssself-serpent."

Adam fell silent. His head was spinning out of control, and his thoughts were overwhelming him with confusion.

Is this for real? Is this really happening?

Adam began to question if he ever really was who he thought he used to be.

Eve has control over me for sure, but when did that creep in?

Eve began to mock and harass the lamb. She was mad at him for interrupting her enjoyment and wanted him to go away, but he just stood there, waiting on Adam to tell him whether or not he was going to return to the Master Gardener.

"Tell him to go away. That is what he is waiting for. He wants to hear it from you, Adam. Just tell him!"

Adam was stricken with guilt and shame. It lay so heavy upon him that he could no longer bear being in the presence of the lamb. He now wanted the lamb to go away too. Therefore, Adam mustered up the strength and told him to go.

The lamb stood there for a minute, and tears began to fill his eyes. As he began to turn to return to the Master Gardener, Eve let out a shout, "Wait! Adam, we cannot let the lamb return to the Master Gardener. The lamb and the Master Gardener will conspire against us. They will be jealous once they know we have chosen to walk our own path and be our own master gardeners. They will try to destroy us, just like the Master Gardener tried to destroy the Tree of the Knowledge of Good and Evil."

"Eve, we have to let him go back."

"No, we don't, Adam. I mean, think about it. Now that we have become our own master gardeners, we can do what we will. We no longer have to do what others will for us. We could cover up all traces of what went on here today. We could get rid of the lamb by silencing him forever."

"Hisss, yesss," the self-serpent agreed.

"What are you talking about, Eve?" Adam asked.

"Here, Adam, I will show you."

Eve grabbed the lamb around its neck. The self-serpent joined in and grabbed him around his back legs.

"Eve! Self-Serpent! What is going on?" Adam yelled.

"Adam, my love, this lamb has been in my business all day. I am now my own master gardener, and I decide who can and who can't be in my business!"

"Eve, think about what you are doing!"

"You think about what you are doing, Adam, and get over here and help me with this lamb!"

Adam had never been forceful with any of the animals. This was a new experience for him, and he was in shock.

"Adam, help me now!"

"How, Eve? How can I help you?"

"Help me tie him up. Let's tie him to the Tree of the Knowledge of Good and Evil, then we can decide how to dispose of him."

It was as if Adam had gone into a trance. His face was void of emotions, and his eyes stayed still. They were open, but as though he were looking off into space.

The self-serpent no longer had to question Eve's thoughts. It just knew. And although the lamb showed no signs of trying to escape, the self-serpent took all precautions. The self-serpent restrained the lamb by coiling around its body and weaving through the lamb's legs. As Eve scurried around looking for something to securely bind the lamb with, Adam noticed the lamb wasn't even trying to escape.

"Why are you being so forceful with him? He is not even trying to get away."

"Here, Adam, I found some vine. Let's tie him up with this."

Shocked and out of his right mind, Adam again listened to the voice of Eve. Together, they both walked the lamb over to the Tree of the Knowledge of Good and Evil and both securely fastened him to it.

Chapter Twenty-Eight

DOUBLE-MINDED ADAM

"Eve, I cannot do this."

"Yes, Adam, you can!"

"I don't think we have been thinking straight, Eve."

"But Adam, that is exactly what we have been doing – thinking straight. And that is why this is so important. We need to come together on this. We need to have one mind in the matter."

Adam was torn between his love's desires and the mental anguish he was experiencing.

"Just think straight with me on this, Adam. After we get rid of the lamb, nothing will stand in our way."

"What do you mean, 'stand in our way'?"

"The lamb obviously didn't obey my commands before. I told him to leave, and he didn't. He is already rebelling against my authority. There is no room for that kind of behavior in our world. Thisss is going to be our life, and we are going to be the rulersss of it."

"But Eve, he was going to leave when you grabbed him. He is not causing us any harm. He is innocent."

"Yes, Adam, but don't you remember what I said? He is the type that will turn against us in our mission to become the best master gardeners we can be."

"I do not remember you quite putting it like that."

"He will go back to the Master Gardener and tell lies about us in order to try and put us back into bondage."

"Bondage?"

"Yes, bondage. The Master Gardener does not care about us. It was a facade. He just wanted to grow us so that He could be our boss, that we could be His slaves. He is the one who wanted to be free, and all the while we were kept under the rule of His strict instructions." Eve sighed. "Oh, Adam, we were always destined to make our own choices and do what we will. If we let the lamb go, we will be letting go of our own freedom. It's time we started taking control of things around here. We were not meant to follow the Master Gardener. We were meant to be the master gardeners of our own selvesss, and we are the ones who determine what that looksss like in our life – not this stupid lamb, or the gardener he reports to."

Adam had become double-minded. While experiencing brief thoughts that Eve might be right, he also wanted her to be wrong. He wanted to focus on the goodness of the Master Gardener, but his mind now raced back and forth between the good and the knowledge of good and evil.

Thoughts of the Master Gardener's love, warmth, protection, and shalom were now raging a war within Adam's being, for he could not stop thinking about the embrace shared with Eve and the self-serpent, nor could he stop himself from wanting to participate in more.

Chapter Twenty-Nine

MORE FREE WILL

Adam was weak more than once on the day of his demise. Not only had he fallen under the temptation of self-pleasure, but now he was full-blown being led by his own self-serpent's desires.

"Eve, can we drink from the Tree of the Knowledge of Good and Evil again? Can we drink from it sssoon?" Adam asked.

"Yesss, my love, we can do it as often as you like, but first, we have business to take care of. We have got to get rid of thisss lamb."

"Okay, but can we please hurry? I am ready to drink some more of itsss juice and tea," Adam urged.

"Yesss, I know, my love."

"Hisss, my new friends," the self-serpent said.

"Hisss," Eve said.

"Hisss hisss ..." Adam said.

The self-serpent was delighted that all three were speaking in one accord.

"Self-serpent, we have business to take care of," Eve said.

"Yesss, I can see. Can I be of assistance?"

"Well, yesss you can. You have been so good to us. Because of you, our eyes are now open to our true potential. I was wondering if you might have any suggestions on how we can get rid of thisss lamb. We are tired of being controlled and feel like he would only be in our way."

"Ah, my dear friends, yesss, I would be glad to share my suggestions. But first, may I ask, what goalsss you want to accomplish in getting rid of the lamb?"

"Well, we truly know that we now can achieve our highest potential. But there is still something standing in our way. We were once weak, being loyal to the Master Gardener. Now that we have set ourselves free, we are no longer weak, and we don't want others in our lives who are. The lamb's loyalty is still with the Master Gardener. Therefore, he is weak and may turn against us. We need to get rid of him for good," Eve said.

"Yesss, my friend. I understand you completely, and I thought thisss might be what you were thinking, but it was good to hear you voice your desssires. We are on the sssame page. Is thisss your desire too, Adam?"

"Yesss, Self-serpent, thisss is my desire too. But please, can we just be quick about thisss? I am ready to drink more of that sssweet tree'sss juice and tea."

"Yesss, my love, we can be quick. I am ready to get thisss over with too. I am ready for thisss lamb to be out of our lives for good," Eve said.

"Yesss, we are all three in agreement and can firmly establish thisss matter. We can get thisss over quickly and move on to bigger and better thingsss," the self-serpent said.

CHAPTER THIRTY

SLAUGHTER OF THE INNOCENT

A dam could not get the previous experience out of his mind. It was as if it had taken him captive and was moving throughout every fiber of his being. He justified what he was about to do, telling himself he wanted to stay one with Eve and drink from the Tree of the Knowledge of Good and Evil.

"Another round, anyone?" the self-serpent asked.

"From the Tree of the Knowledge of Good and Evil?" Adam and Eve both asked.

"Yesss, I remembered how enjoyable it was for you earlier," the self-serpent said.

"Thank you, Self-serpent, how thoughtful of you!" Eve said.

"I have an idea, my friends. It is an answer to your question: *Do I have any sssuggestions concerning how you may get rid of the lamb?*"

"Yesss, Self-serpent, let us hear it," Eve said.

"We are lissstening," Adam added.

"It is no secret to us how enjoyable our prior moments together were. We should partake again and have another moment like our previous one. Partaking in the Tree of the Knowledge of Good and Evil once more will remove our inhibitions, and at that point, we will be at our highest. Disposing of the lamb will then come easy for us," the self-serpent said.

"Soundsss like a plan to me," Eve responded.

Both the self-serpent and Eve turned towards Adam as if to look for his response.

Eve was caught off guard by Adam's changed countenance, but she didn't question it. She was determined to see their plan through.

"I'm game!" Adam yelled as he threw his head back and started laughing an eerie laugh. From that point forward, Adam no longer seemed anything like his old self. "Draw near, my love. Draw near, Self-serpent," he went on. "I want some more of that deliciousss drink to enjoy with my female ..."

As Adam was speaking, he grabbed Eve by the arm and harshly drew her to himself. "I want more!" he yelled.

Eve didn't appreciate his roughness.

"Hey, not so rough!" she squealed.

"Oh, you know you like it," Adam said.

"Yesss! I believe she does," the self-serpent said.

"Wait, the lamb!" Eve yelled.

"Yesss, the lamb," the self-serpent responded.

Adam gave a huge eye roll and released Eve from his forced embrace.

"Okay, I've got this," Adam said.

Eve froze. She was trying to read Adam's countenance but was having a hard time doing so.

"Adam, are you okay?"

"Yesss, Eve, I am better than ever. Stay here with the lamb. I will be right back."

"I will ssstay too," the self-serpent said.

Eve had no clue about the depravity that Adam was experiencing, but the self-serpent was *not* clueless and knew what Adam was thinking.

I most certainly will ssstay right here with the lamb and Eve. Although he is tied to thisss tree, I want to make sure Eve does not let him get away.

Adam hastily went from standing near the tree trunk where the lamb was tied, to near one of its low-hanging branches.

"No, not thisss one, it is not sharp enough," he said, and then moved on to begin examining another.

"Ah! Here it is. Thisss one will do."

"Adam, what are you doing?" Eve asked.

"Thisss should be sharp enough to get the job done," he said.

Adam snapped off one of the tree's sharp branches and returned to Eve, the self-serpent, and the innocent lamb.

As he walked back, Eve noticed that not only had Adam's countenance changed, but also his expression had become very fierce. This greatly concerned her, but by then, she had also become weak and entrapped by her own lustful desires for power.

"Hold him tight, Eve!" Adam yelled.

"I've got him!" she responded.

"No, tighter!"

"I have the vine around his neck as tight as it will go, Adam! I cannot get it any tighter!" she yelled.

"His legsss are sssecure! He is not going anywhere!" the self-serpent said.

"Okay, now hold him still," Adam said.

"Hisss, don't forget your mixed drink!" the self-serpent said.

"Yesss, the mixed drink! I am ready!" Adam said.

Adam had the sharp tree branch in one hand and the mixed drink in his other. He drank and then passed the cup to Eve.

"Save some for the lamb," he said.

"The lamb?" she asked curiously.

"Yesss, the lamb."

Although the lamb was tied to the tree, Eve still held on to him tightly. Pushing his neck up against the tree with the force of her body, she carefully held the cup, being careful not to spill it.

"You want me to save some drink for the lamb? Did I hear you right?"

"Yesss, you heard me right. Save some drink for the lamb. He needs to partake with us."

By this time, Adam had become deranged-looking. It frightened Eve, but she had come too far in the situation to ask any questions. Lifting the cup and drinking her portion while leaning in towards the lamb – whose neck was tied to the tree and legs were being held by the self-serpent – Eve managed to force the rest of the drink down the lamb's throat.

"Yesss, hisss ... Victory!" the self-serpent exclaimed.

Tears began to well up in Eve's eyes and she was reminded of the first time she drank from the tree.

"My eyes teared up then too," she said quietly under her breath.

The lamb began to sweat profusely.

Suddenly, the once-silent lamb let out a grievous moan. Adam had pierced its body with the sharp branch he had chosen from the Tree of the Knowledge of Good and Evil. Blood and water began to spew out, and it was everywhere.

Adam and Eve had never seen blood before. Some even splattered on their faces and entered their mouths, causing them to experience the taste of it. And as they tasted, they enjoyed it, and did drink more.

The lamb's body soon stopped breathing and he became lifeless. Adam and Eve began to howl with excitement. They raised their hands and jumped for joy in wild ecstasy. As they celebrated their success in getting rid of their problem, looking forward to feasting on the Tree of the Knowledge of Good and Evil, everything suddenly went dark.

Chapter Thirty-One

DARKNESS FELL UPON THE SET-APART PLACE

"Adam!" Eve yelled.

"Eve!" Adam yelled back.

"Adam! Adam, where are you? I cannot see you! Where are you, my love?!" Eve was beginning to panic.

"I am close, my love. Stay calm. Extend your arm out and I will find you."

Eve extended her arm into the dark unknown.

"I am here, my love, come close and please hurry," she said.

Adam had his arms extended out too, but because everything was dark, he had to rely on Eve's voice in order to find her, which he eventually did.

"Oh, Adam, I am so scared. What is happening? What is going on?"

"I know as much as you do, Eve! Now hush! We have to remain calm."

Although Adam was instructing Eve to stay calm, he was nowhere near that.

"Self-serpent! Self-serpent, are you there?" he yelled.

"Oh, come closer, my love, please hold me closer," Eve said.

"I am holding you as close as I can."

"Ow! That hurts, Adam!"

"You told me to hold you closer!"

"I didn't mean so tightly! That hurts!"

"I didn't mean to hurt you!"

Both Adam and Eve had lost all evidence of shalom. It was nowhere to be found.

"I'm sorry, I just didn't want to lose you. It's so dark, but I am sorry if I hurt you," he said.

"Adam, what is going on? I am so cold, and I cannot see you! Where have you gone, my love?"

"I have not gone anywhere. I am right here holding you. And I do not know what is going on either, Eve!"

"But I don't see your light. I don't see anything. It's so dark, Adam!"

"I know that, Eve! I know that it is dark!"

Both Adam and Eve were trembling. Fear had consumed their beings. Their inner lights were no longer lit, and the Greater Light was no longer shining.

"Adam, I'm scared. What is happening?"

"I told you I don't know, Eve! I don't know any more than you do! Now please, just stop with the questions!"

"Self-serpent! Where are you?" Adam shouted.

"Self-serpent! Why have you left us?" Eve added.

"Self-serpent!" Adam yelled again.

"Oh, Adam! Something is so wrong. I am really scared."

"Me too, Eve."

"What are we going to do?"

"I don't know! Why do you think I have the answers to your questions? I have never experienced this before either!"

Eve began to sob.

"Here, give me your hand. Let's just find a place where we can sit down and think a minute. Maybe our inner lights will come back if we just calm down," Adam said.

"What about the Greater Light? It's gone too, Adam. And the star lights, they don't appear to be shining!"

"I know that, Eve! Do you think that I cannot tell? Why do you keep repeating yourself?"

Eve began to sob uncontrollably. She was in such a fright that her grip on Adam's being began to be uncomfortable for him.

"Lighten up. Now you are the one with the grip that's hurting me."

Eve lessened her grip slightly.

"Here, let's just sit here a minute," Adam said.

Eve continued to whimper.

"My hair is matted, Adam!"

"What? What are you talking about?"

"Adam! You are pulling my hair, stop it, please!"

"Oh, I am sorry, my love. I was just trying to hold on to all of you."

Eve started to panic again.

"Well, please just let go of my hair. It's a tangled mess! What is going on, Adam? I am a mess; I am a tangled mess! I can't see you! Your light is gone, mine is gone too! Oh, Adam ..."

"Hush, my love, just hush!"

"Okay, Adam, I am trying. I am really trying!"

Holding on to each other, Adam and Eve shook from dreadful fright. This went on for what seemed like a very long time, until they both passed out from shock and exhaustion.

Some time later, Adam woke up and looked around. He could see clearly again.

"Eve! It's back! It's back! The Greater Light is back on!"

"It is!"

"Ah, Eve! I am so grateful!"

"But Adam, when are *our* lights going to come back on? I still don't see yours, and I don't imagine you can see mine."

"I don't see yours, my love."

"Oh, Adam, when do you think they will return?"

"I don't know, my love. I don't know. Maybe they will come back on soon," he said.

"Maybe so."

Adam's and Eve's lights were not the only things that were gone. Their joy and innocence were gone too. They both felt like they had entered a nightmare, except this was no nightmare.

With the Greater Light shining again, the reality of what had taken place overwhelmed Adam with anguish. He released Eve from their embrace and began to look around at all the mess.

There is blood everywhere, he thought.

"That's what matted your hair. It's his blood, Eve! His blood is all through your hair. It's on your face. It's all on me too, in my hair and on my face, on my being and on my hands!"

Eve had never heard Adam speak in such regret and anguish. She was at a loss and didn't know how to respond. Seeing the lamb lying lifeless at its slaughter place, there was no denying they were covered in its blood.

Eve tried to reach out to Adam, but he would not be consoled.

"Stop! Don't touch me!"

Eve began to cry.

"Hush! Just hush, Eve!"

"But Adam!"

"No buts, Eve! Look at this place! Look around you! Can you see? Can you see what we have done? Do you see all the blood? Do you see the lamb? He's dead, Eve! He is dead! And his blood is on our hands!"

Eve moved slightly forward to try to embrace Adam, but she was abruptly stopped by the slap of his hand across the side of her face.

"Don't even try it, Eve. I told you not to touch me. Just get away from me, you dirty, filthy rag! Do you hear me? Get away from me!"

Eve brought her hand up and touched the side of her face where Adam had slapped her. She stood there for several minutes in shock, not knowing what to do next.

CHAPTER THIRTY-TWO

FIG LEAVES FOR THE FALLEN

"Here, hold these fig leaves," Adam said.

"What are you going to do with them?" Eve asked.

"Quit asking so many questions. Just do as I say."

Eve was not used to Adam speaking with her in that tone of voice, nor had she been asking a lot of questions since he had slapped her. But, at this point, she did not dare go to battle against him.

Stop asking questions, Eve! Not even one! Just do what he says, she thought.

Eve was beginning to realize the magnitude of the predicament they were both in. And she was now realizing just how much she needed her male.

"It is going to be a covering, Eve. A covering for the nakedness of our shame. Now here, hold these while I weave this vine through them."

Adam finished weaving the vine throughout the first bunch of fig leaves, making the first covering. He then tied a vine around Eve's waistline and sewed the covering to it, leaving it to hang over the area of her being where she had participated in the violations.

"Now you do the same for me," Adam said.

Eve tied a vine around Adam's waistline, repeating the process. He, too, was then covered in the area of his being where the violations had taken place.

Chapter Thirty-Three

IN THE COOL OF THE DAY

"What is that?" a trembling Eve asked. "The wind is beginning to pick up, and I hear a rustling in the leaves. It's headed this way."

Eve had never before been frightened by the sounds of nature. But today was different. She no longer held shalom in her being, for fear and anxiety had consumed her.

"Don't you know?" Adam said in a strong but low voice.

Eve started crying again.

"It is Him, Eve! It is the Master Gardener! He must be looking for us since I never went to our meeting."

"Looking for us?"

"Yes, Eve! Looking for us! What is with you? Why can't you get a clue? You really aren't that smart, are you?"

How did things get so bad, so quickly? How did we fall so far from what once was? I miss my kind Adam. Will he ever look at me the same? she thought.

"Here, let us go this way. We can take this path to the aspen trees and hide from Him there," Adam said.

Eve knew that Adam was tired of her questions, but she couldn't help herself.

"How long do you think we can hide from Him?"

By this point, Adam was so fed up with Eve's presence that he hurried on ahead of her.

"Adam, wait! Please don't leave me!" Eve pleaded.

Other than an eye roll, Adam didn't respond – he just kept walking ahead of her, so fast that it looked like he was leaving her.

"Hurry up," he yelled back her way.

"I am coming! Hold on!"

Adam stopped for a moment and allowed Eve to catch up.

He pointed off to the side. "Let us go this way. We can get lost in the trees here," he said.

Nightfall was closing in on them.

"It is cold, Adam. I have never been so cold before. I have experienced being cool before, but never so cold. Do you think the aspen trees are what make this forest so cold? It's way colder here than the rest of the Set-Apart Place," she said.

"It is our lights, Eve! Our inner lights are gone. That is why you are so cold."

"Aren't you cold too, Adam?"

"Yes, Eve! I am cold too! With the Greater Light setting, the temperature feels like it is dropping. We no longer have our inner lights to warm us through the darkness, at least until they are turned back on. We are just going have to deal with it!"

"Do you think they will ever come back on?"

Adam was becoming frustrated again.

"I don't know!" he exclaimed.

Adam and Eve were huddled together in a burrow they had dug when the Master Gardener spotted them.

"There you are!" the Master Gardener said as He began to walk toward them. "I am really glad I found you!"

Both Adam and Eve were sorely afraid. They shook from fearful dread. Neither one wanted to be found, let alone have to face the Master Gardener.

"Hello, My dear children. Didn't you hear My voice?" the Master Gardener asked.

Adam's and Eve's heads were hanging low. They continued to avoid responding to the Master Gardener, until Adam could no longer hold on to his shame.

"Hello, Master Gardener, we are here," he said.

"Yes, I know, but what are you doing here? And why didn't you respond to My voice? What is this mess you have gotten yourself covered in? It has dimmed your light, and it was hard to recognize you. You are a mess, both of you. And Eve, your beautiful hair! Adam, tell me what has happened."

"I heard Your voice and was afraid, Master Gardener. We both were," Adam said.

"Of Me?" the Master Gardener asked.

"Yes, of You, Master Gardener."

"Well, My child, healthy fear is honorable, but hiding fear is not. Why did you hide from Me?" the Master Gardener asked.

Adam's being was shaking uncontrollably on the inside and out.

"Um, well, Master Gardener, I was naked and I felt ashamed. Therefore, I hid from you."

"Who told you that you were naked? Have you eaten from the Tree of the Knowledge of Good and Evil?" the Master Gardener asked, a shocked expression appearing on His face.

All Adam could do was stand there and tremble and think about how mad he was at Eve for getting him into this situation.

"Eve made me do it, Master Gardener!" he blurted. "It is her fault! She said that if I would just listen to her, then we could become our own master gardeners. And Master Gardener, I did. I did listen to her. And now I know I should not have, but if You had never made her for me, then I would not be in this predicament."

"Predicament?" the Master Gardener asked.

"Yes, Master Gardener, this predicament."

"Explain that to me. Adam, what predicament have you found yourself in?"

"I have done a horrible thing, Master Gardener. I know it is Eve's fault, for she made me do it."

Eve began to interrupt in order to speak up for herself, but the Master Gardener was not having it.

"Hush! You will have your turn shortly. Carry on, Adam."

"Eve said that if we drank the juice of the fruit of the Tree of the Knowledge of Good and Evil that it would cause us to become limitless and we could then become our own master gardeners. She drank it before me and then persuaded me to drink. I did, and it caused me to do awful things, Master Gardener, very awful things. But it is her fault, Master Gardener! Why did You make her for me? She has led me astray!"

"That is enough, Adam. Eve, come here," the Master Gardener said.

Eve stood and came forward. Her head hung low. "It was the self-serpent, Master Gardener. It deceived me into listening to its voice, and I did listen. I am sorry, Master Gardener! I am so sorry! Please forgive me!"

Both Adam and Eve stood there before the Master Gardener. Their inner lights were gone. They were filthy from the blood that stained their once beautiful and dignified beings. They were guilty, naked, and ashamed. Both talked with the Master Gardener for hours into the night. And just before the Greater Light began to rise, the Master Gardener painstakingly walked them towards the Fence-of-Fire, leading them to exit the Set-Apart Place.

Eve's head was spinning. She would have been comforted by the warmth of the Fence-of-Fire if it had not been for her circumstances. She was cold, miserable, and tired.

"Please, Master Gardener, please – isn't there another way?" she begged.

The Master Gardener's countenance was greatly grieved. Huge tears ran down His face as He answered her:

"This is the other way, My child."

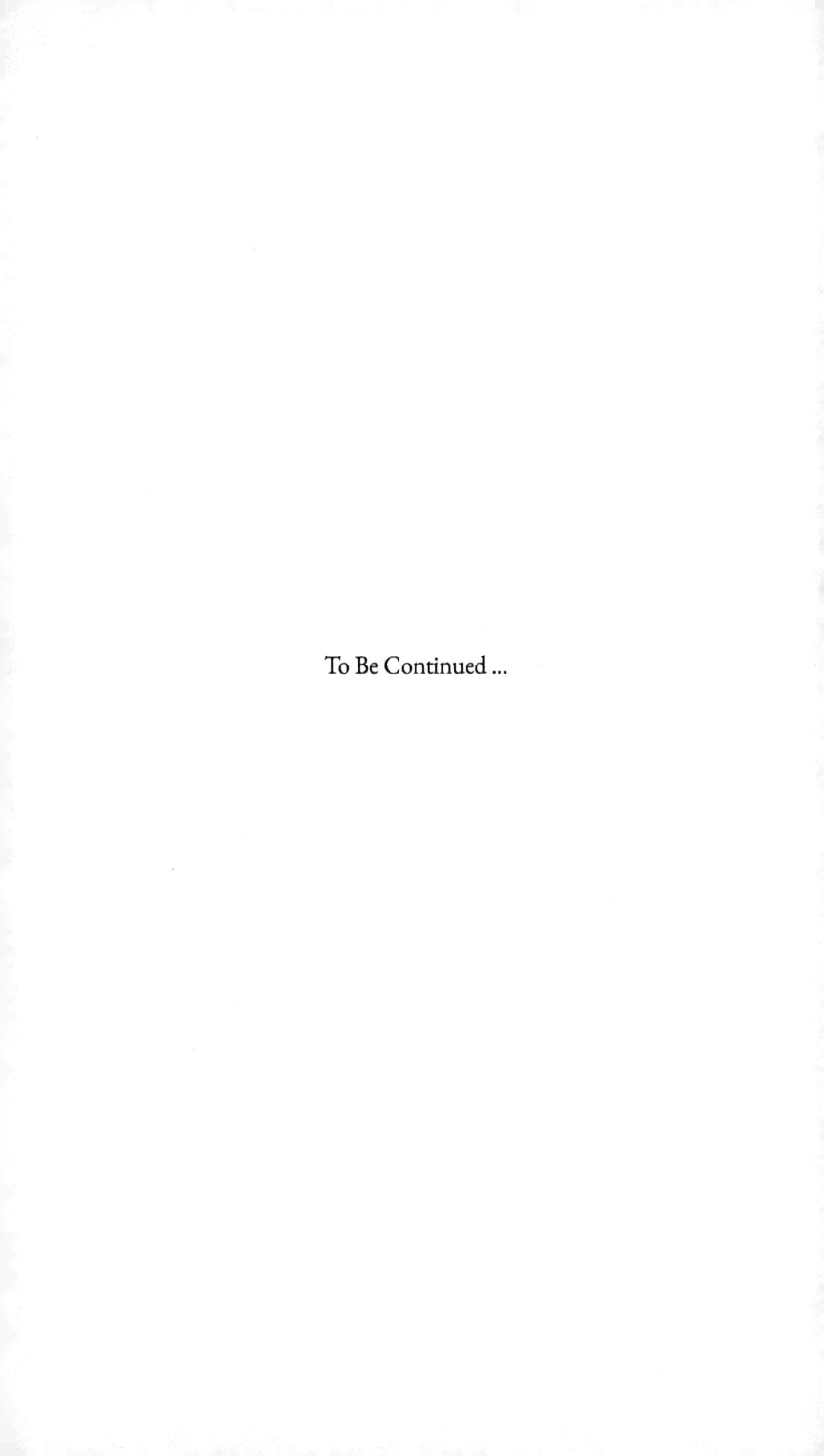

To Be Continued ...

By their own actions, Adam and Eve are cast out of the Master's garden, throwing them into a wilderness journey of refinement. Knowing that they cannot return to the most beautiful and set-apart place in all the Earth, they must trek forward and forge on. Facing many trials along their journey, both fumble around in the shadows of what once was.

Will their hearts ever recover? Will they ever be able to experience true joy again? Author Brandi Danielle answers these questions and more in **Fallen Nature**, the next book in **The Set-Apart Place** series. For updates on the series, please visit http://brandidanielle.blog